# SWEET TALES

**ANONYMOUS**

Carroll & Graf Publishers, Inc.
New York

Copyright © 1990 by Carroll & Graf Publishers, Inc
All rights reserved

First Carroll & Graf edition 1990

Carroll & Graf Publishers, Inc.
260 Fifth Avenue
New York, NY 10001

ISBN: 0-88184-606-6

Manufactured in the United States of America

# Part I

# CONTENTS

# CHAPTER I

## WHAT THE NUNS NEEDED

CELIBACY, as it is enjoined in the Roman Church, is not only unwise as being opposed to nature, but it is provocative of the very evils that it is intended to banish and destroy.

Some individuals may have a spiritual gift in that way, but in the greater number of cases, young people, before they understand their nature or themselves, are induced, by reason of their emotional feelings being stirred up and directed by the Church, to take upon themselves vows which, when too late, they find it utterly impossible to carry out.

These emotional feelings are evanescent in their character, and are easily overpowered, either by the strong natural instinct of propagation, which becomes developed in most people as they grow to

1

maturity, or when they are brought into contact with temptations of a lascivious tendency. And these very temptations, strange to say, they are sure to meet with sooner or later in the confessional.

There are abundant historical proofs of the truth of these statements in every country where that form of religion has prevailed; and nowhere more than in Italy, its great centre, and also among the ecclesiastics and religious bodies which there abound.

The following story, the facts of which are well authenticated, affords an interesting and amusing illustration.

There was, in the suburbs of a northern city, a handsome building, with well-kept gardens and grounds. This house was occupied by a sisterhood of nuns under the care of a Mother Abbess. She was a titled lady by birth, and in her younger days had been married to an old man. She was naturally of a voluptuous disposition, and not being satisfied by her husband, consoled herself in the arms of a young noble of their acquaintance. On one occasion they were surprised in the very act by her husband. The aged man made a furious onslaught on her gallant. In defending himself the younger man unfortunately ran him through with his rapier. The affair caused such scandal, and she, to make the best amend she could, took the veil, and retired into a convent. She had a brother, a Bishop; and by his influence and her own energy and talents, she was gradually promoted, until now, in her thirty-fifth year, she was made a Mother Abbess. She had under her charge twenty-four nuns, chiefly of her own selection. They were all good-looking young women, with the exception of four, who, being elderly, were chosen as examples of sanctity and strict adherence to convent rules and discipline.

The grounds and gardens were kept in order by an old man who slept outside the Convent bounds. He had managed to scrape together a little money, and at the time of our story felt that his years unfitted him for his work; and so he resolved to resign his post, and pass the remainder of his days in quiet and ease.

The position was a good and lucrative one, and was sought after by many. Among others was a nephew of the old gardener's named Tasso, who wished to obtain it. He possessed good qualifications for the post, as he had been trained on the property of a nobleman in the South, but he was a comparative stranger in the district in which the Convent was situated. He requested his uncle to recommend him, but the old man assured him that

3

it would be of no use, for the objection would be that he was young, well-made, and altogether too good-looking; and he knew that the Mother Abbess, who prided herself on the reputation for sanctity which the Convent had acquired, would in all probability decline to engage anyone but a man, tolerably old, and not so prepossessing in appearance.

"And she is right," he added, "for among the holy Sisters are some young women that seem to me to be ready for almost any sort of mischief, – and from the way I have seen them sporting with one another, when they thought they were unobserved, I think that under their sober vestal garb they have as skittish natures as any girls I have ever seen."

This only made young Tasso all the more eager; for, like the war horse, he smelled the battle from afar, and his blood warmed for the fray.

"Well, uncle," he replied. "Don't oppose me. Give me your consent, and let me endeavour by my own wits to induce the Mother Abbess to give me at least a fair trial."

Now Tasso was not only a young man of enterprise, but he was also singularly intelligent and wise in his generation. With great craft he determined to represent himself as being deaf and dumb, and to assume a heavy and stolid appearance. By what arts he persuaded his uncle to give him the desired recommendation, and by what means he obtained the old man's promise of secrecy, history does not tell us. We only know that when he went to the Mother Abbess with a note of introduction from his uncle, he had artfully disguised as much as possible his good looks and youthful appearance, and he communicated with her by means of a slate which he carried with him, and on which she wrote her questions to him and he replied in fairly legible writing.

She was pleased with the recommendations he had, and pitied his infirmities, but was rather repelled by his uncouth manner and unkempt hair; but on considering the matter she thought that after all, his not being very inviting in appearance, and especially his being deaf and dumb, might be of great advantage, as it would certainly render him less communicative either inside or outside the Convent.

So she finally engaged him on a month's trial.

Upon the following day Tasso entered on his duties. He knew his business well, and apparently thought of nothing else.

Now it was the custom of the Sisters to take exercise at certain hours in the Convent grounds. They looked at him in a friendly way, and some of them made bold to speak a few kind words. But to these advances he would always reply by a shake of his head, at the same time pointing to his ears and lips. Then he would hold out his slate, – which, when not in use, he carried in his pocket, – for them to write any commands they wished to give. But the Mother Abbess, ever on the watch, soon saw that he made no attempt to communicate with them of his own accord; and convinced that this was the right man for the place at last, and relying on his simplicity, she relaxed her vigilance, and gave her attention to more pressing duties.

After a while, the Sisters realized that he was deaf and dumb, and seemed to forget his presence, talking to one another just as if he was not there at all.

They thought him stupid as well as deaf, but all the while he kept his eyes open and his ears attentive, so that nothing passed unnoticed that came within their reach. Soon he had learned the names of all the Sisters, and could recognize them by their voices.

Two of the younger nuns, Lucia and Robina, seemed to have taken a fancy to him, for they often walked near where he was at work, and always gave him a smile as they passed.

There were many rustic seats scattered about, in shady spots, and these were much used by the nuns in their hours of recreation.

Whenever Tasso was occupied near any of these seats, the Sisters Lucia and Robina were sure to come and sit there and watch him, while they talked or worked at their embroidery.

Their usual conversation was of convent matters, such as their work or their teaching, – for nearly all the nuns took part in the instruction of the young ladies who attended the Convent School.

But on one occasion they commenced to talk of their Confessors. Lucia declared that she liked Father Joachim best, for he seemed to take more interest in the Convent.

"Only," she added, "He does ask such bothering questions."

"What kind of questions?" asked Robina, with a smile.

"Why, Sister! Don't you know we're not allowed to tell anything outside the confessional of what takes place within? However, you and I are such friends that we may disregard these hard rules when we are talking confidentially together, – may we not?"

"Yes, certainly. Go on."

Here Tasso, who appeared to be very busy,

7

moved a little nearer, and worked noiselessly.

"Well, the other night I had a queer dream. I had been looking, during the day, at a fine picture of St. Martin, painted by Titian; and when I was asleep, I thought that I saw him coming towards me with no clothing on at all, and Oh! he looked so very beautiful. As he advanced, I saw something between his legs, though I cannot tell you what it was like. But while I was looking at it, he came up and lay down over me. And I thought I felt his body pressing mine in a most delightful way, and I got a delicious feeling in the corresponding part of myself. Then I suddenly awoke, and – what do you think? I had one of my fingers pushed right up into myself, and I could not stop rubbing it in and out until I became all wet. Since then I have put my hand there several times, and it always gives me great pleasure. Now, of course, I know this is all very wrong, and I had to confess it to the priest."

"And what were his bothering questions?"

"Oh! He made me describe exactly where my finger was. I had to tell him, it was in my woman's slit, between the soft lips that we have there. Then he asked what was it I saw between St. Martin's legs, and if I knew what it was for? I felt annoyed at such a question, and said, 'How could I tell? I suppose it was what all men have there.'

8

"Then he asked, for these holy Fathers never seem to feel abashed, if I ever thought about a man's part, and whether I had any longing to see it, and know what it was like?

"I confessed that I had felt some curiosity about it, but that I always tried to banish such thoughts from my mind.

"He said that it was quite right, that such thoughts were natural to both men and women, and all that was required was not to allow them to dwell in the mind. Then he told me to come to him soon again, and tell him all my thoughts, and that he would hear my confession in the Mother Abbess' private room. Since then I have been thinking more than ever about these very things; and do you know, Robina, I have quite a longing to know what a man's thing is like? Haven't you?"

"Sometimes, dear. But it is very likely that Father Joachim may gratify your longing himself. I fancy he has some such intention in his mind, and that's why he said he would hear your confession in the Mother Abbess' private room. Meantime, let me tell you that these lusty priests use the confessional as a means of gratifying their own sensual desires. They know that we poor nuns are quite in their power, and they dearly love to make us tell them every secret thought which naturally comes

9

into our minds as women, with regard to the other sex. And more than that, they often suggest the thoughts themselves, and when we are at a loss, they supply the words too. It does seem strange to me, if these things are as wicked as they declare in their public teaching, why they encourage them so directly in their secret ministrations in the confessional. Now I'll tell you, Lucia, what I shall propose: Let us be true to one another; and consult together to get all the fun we can out of these holy Fathers, and at the same time enjoy any little pleasure that comes in our way, for indeed ours is a hard lot."

"I quite agree with you, dear Robina," said Lucia, "and gladly accept your proposal, for I too am heartily sick of the tiresome round of these vigils, fasts, prayers and penances, which instead of making us better, only drive us to something worse, as a mere matter of relief. We never see anything in the shape of a man, except these oily priests, with their sensual mouths and wicked-looking eyes. Somehow I don't trust them, and I can't abide them. Now there is some comfort in looking at this poor, honest, hard-working fellow, Tasso. And, Robina, have you noticed how well made he is? Look at his nicely-turned limbs!"

"You are right, Lucia," replied Robina.

"There is some satisfaction in looking at him. And indeed I was just thinking that, if we could see him as you saw St. Martin in your dream, we should behold a very satisfactory illustration of that special part which is most interesting to us as women. Is that what you were thinking of, you rogue?"

And looking at her with glittering eyes, she gave her a nudge with her elbow.

Lucia laughed merrily.

"Why not, my dear? Father Joachim says that such thoughts are only natural; and as we are forever shut off from the reality, it cannot be so very wrong for us to console ourselves with the thought."

"Quite so," replied Robina. "But let me tell you a notion which has come into my head, I don't know how. May we not try at least to turn our thought into reality? Could we not manage to induce Tasso in some way to gratify our curiosity? He is so simple that I am sure he would think nothing of showing all he has to us, if we could but make him feel that we would neither be frightened nor affronted, nor tell anyone. Now what do you think of that notion, Lucia?"

"Capital, dear! But how can it be brought about?"

"I'll tell you one way that we might obtain our

object even without his knowledge. I noticed yesterday when one of the Sisters brought him a glass of our light wine as a reward for moving her rose-trees so nicely, that after he drank it, he stole away among the laurels near our Little-house, (a name they had for a place of convenience in a corner of the grounds,) and I fancy he went there to make water. Now it occurs to me that if one of us got him some drink this hot day, and the other went to hide in the Little-house, she would have a chance of getting a view of that part of him which we would both like to see, and then she could tell the other all that occurred."

"You are very clever, Sister Robina," replied Lucia, "and you know many things of which I am ignorant. I cordially approve of your plan, and if you will place yourself in ambush in the Little-house, I will run for the drink. – But mind! You must describe to me afterwards everything you have seen, with the greatest precision."

"All right! Let us go away together, and I will steal round to the hiding-place without his seeing me."

Tasso fairly grinned with delight. His crafty device was already bearing fruit, and his manly organ bounded with exultation at the thought of anticipated triumph.

Lucia quickly reappeared with a cup brimming with love-inspiring drink. He took it from her hands with a grateful nod, and immediately drank it off. On receiving the cup again, she turned away to bring it back to the house. Tasso at once made off to the corner indicated, and having placed himself in full view before the door, which was pierced with holes for the purpose of ventilation, he took out his middle limb, and exhibited its full length and even the large appendages beneath. It was a splendid specimen of a flesh-coloured prick, large and strong, in the full flush of youthful power and beauty. Holding it in his hand, he made his water shoot out before him in a way that could not fail to be most interesting to a female observer. Then he drew down the soft white skin so as to uncover all the glowing head, now of a bright rosy tint. He shook it from side to side until the last amber drop had fallen, and then, as if yielding to some sudden impulse, he began to imitate the common fucking motion by vigorously working his posteriors and making his prick pass swiftly backwards and forwards through his hands.

The hidden watcher eyes it with the same regard a famished wolf has for a tempting morsel. Her bosoms heave and swell like the ocean billows scurrying before the storm. In vain she grasps

13

them with her hands. In vain she tries to calm the rapid tumultuous beating of her heart. Her breath comes quickly. It is frequently interrupted by the soft sighs which escape her. Something within her seems to jump, and then a flame devours her. Instinctively one hand strays from throbbing bosom down to her robe. The black garb is quickly drawn up, and her hand touches the mossy charms beneath. Passion's hottest fires are already flaming furiously. Yonder, in the thicket, is the only solace that will afford her relief. Ah! If she only had it in her grasp! A rosy mist floats before her eyes. In its very midst, surrounded by a golden halo, she sees the gardener's own tool, – the glorious badge of manhood that Tasso alone possesses. Its ruby head turns toward her. Look! It quivers with passion. A few pearly drops ooze from it, glitter in the sunlight, and fall. Then the vision fades from her view.

For, with a faint sigh of satisfaction, Tasso has pushed it in under cover again, and has buttoned up his trousers. And the crunch of gravel under his feet a moment later informs the passionate girl that Tasso is returning to his work.

# CHAPTER II

## HOW THEY OBTAINED IT

TASSO'S great hope was that the two Sisters would return to their seat, and favour him a little more by their delightful conversation. Nor was he disappointed. The Sisters quickly reappeared, and bringing with them their embroidery, sat down in the seat they had occupied before.

Tasso was conscious that they now regarded him with peculiar interest, and that their eyes looked as if they were trying to penetrate that portion of his attire. He therefore pushed it out and made it prominent as much as he could.

Lucia was speaking.

"Well, Robina, you certainly had a grand success. How I envy you! It must have been delightful to watch him, when he thought he was all alone, first piddling and then actually playing with his thing! But now, tell me, like a good dear, exactly what it was like: its size, its colour, and above, all, tell me its shape."

"You must try and see it yourself, my dear," replied Robina, "for it is not an easy thing to describe. It seemed about eight inches long, and nearly as thick as your wrist, but quite round. It is covered with a soft white skin which slips easily up and down. When he pulled this skin back, the top stood up like a large round head, shelving to a point, and of a purplish red colour. It was that which attracted me most, and, my dear, it had a most wonderful effect on myself. My hairy slit began to thrill and to throb in such a way that, for the life of me, I could not help pulling up my dress and rubbing it with my hand. And it grew hotter and hotter, until a warm flow came, and gave me relief."

"What a delightful time you must have had, Robina," commented Lucia. "Do you know your telling me all this has made mine frightfully hot, too?" And she twisted about, rubbing her bottom on the seat. "How I wish Tasso was not watching us. I would ask you to put your kind hand on my slit and afford me a little of the same pleasure."

Robina laughed.

"I fancy he's not thinking of us at all. He is too

16

dull to have any notions of that kind. Stand up, dear, as if you were pulling some buds from the branch overhanging us, and I will slip my hand up from behind, so that he can see nothing. Now, do you like that, dear?"

"Oh! Your fingers are giving me great pleasure!" replied the excited Lucia. "There! That's the place! – Push it up! – Oh! Wouldn't it be nice to have Tasso's delightful thing poking me there! – You said, Robina, that was Nature's intention, and that the mutual touch of our differently formed parts gives the greatest satisfaction. What fools we were to give it up!"

"What a child you are, Lucia! The holy Fathers will teach you that you may enjoy it now more than ever, and without doing anything wrong, either, only it must be done with them alone."

"Now! Oh! Now, Robina! – Push your finger up! As far as you can! How I long for Tasso's dear thing! – Oh! Oh! – That will do!"

And she sat down, and leaned her head against Robina for support.

It will be easily understood what an overpowering effect this scene had on poor Tasso. His sturdy prick, glowing with youthful vigour, seemed to be trying to break its covering and burst into open view.

17

The unsuspecting talk of the two Sisters almost maddened him. He felt that if he could only present his "dear thing," as they called it, openly before them, he might obtain from one or the other, or from perhaps both, the sweet favour he desired.

In this mood he gradually worked up close to them, and slyly unbuttoned his clothes down the front.

He restrained himself, however, for the present, that he might learn something more from the Sisters, who went on talking.

"But Robina, what shall we do about confessing this touching of ourselves and one another to the priests? If we conceal it, our confession is incomplete and sinful, as they tell us we ought to make a full avowal of all our faults and shortcomings. You know how they are always urging this upon us as a sacred duty. And if we give him the slightest hint, Father Joachim will be sure to worm out from us all about Tasso, and that might do him much harm, and cause him to be sent away, – and we too may be separated, and not allowed to walk with one another."

"Quite true, Lucia. We must do all we can to guard against these two evils. And there really is no way but to keep the whole matter a secret between ourselves. I, for my part, won't let that press upon my conscience, as I now know that there is so much humbug and deceit about the confessional that I have no faith in it as a religious duty at all."

"I am with you again, Robina," replied Lucia. "It would be an awful wrong to injure poor Tasso, who is quite innocent; and if you and I were separated, – why, I should die, and that would be the end of it."

Tasso was greatly pleased at hearing this, for his mind was now satisfied that so far as these two Sisters were concerned, he had no cause to dread exposure and its certain consequences.

"Well, Lucia, dear, we'll try to prevent that, at all events. We shall have to go to the priest, but we must carefully avoid all reference to anyone but ourselves. It will be great fun, I am sure, to confess our looking at and petting our own slits. We can tell him our dreams also. That will sufficiently please him, and perhaps draw him on to commit himself with us, and then he will have to keep quiet for his own sake."

And they both laughed at the thought.

Just then, a little accident happened to Tasso which gave a sudden turn to their conversation. As he was bending at his work, his foot slipped, and he rolled over on his back. This motion, in the most natural way, set his prick free, and it started out, looking very stiff and inflamed.

He quickly jumped up, and looking at his naked prick with stupid amazement, began to utter uncouth sounds, like an ordinary donkey: "Hoo! Awe!" And he made some ineffectual attempts to push it back into its place.

"There! Lucia," cried Robina. "Your wish is granted. This poor simple fellow has accidentally given you the view for which you were longing. Don't you admire it?"

"Yes! – But what should we do, Robina, if any of the Sisters were to come up now? What a hubbub there would be! – But see! – I declare, he can't get it back."

"Well, go and help him, Lucia. Make haste, and I will keep a lookout."

Lucia's eyes were intently fastened on the interesting object. Her face was flushed, and she looked altogether extremely excited. She had no time however, for reflection. So she jumped up, as her friend advised, went to Tasso, and tried to help to get his rebellious tool back into its hiding-place.

Taking advantage of his apparent simplicity, and wishing to expedite matters, she took hold of his prick with her hand.

But Oh! How the touch of that piece of animated flesh thrilled her! It felt so warm and soft, yet so firm and strong! She could neither bend it, nor push it back. And the more she made the effort, the more strongly did it resist and stand out.

"Oh! dear! Oh! dear! What shall I do, Robina? It won't go back for me!"

Robina laughed until the tears ran down her cheeks.

"Anyway, take him along," she replied. "Bring him into the summer-house."

This happened to be conveniently near, and was well screened by bushes. Lucia with a smile, pointed it out to Tasso, and still holding his prick, gently drew him on.

Tasso, putting on a most innocent look, went readily with her, and Robina followed in the rear.

As they entered the leafy shade, she said: "Now, Lucia, you have him all to yourself. If you don't succeed in getting him to do every thing you want, you are a less clever girl than I take you to be. If all else fails, just show him your mossy nest, and that will draw him as surely as a magnet attracts a piece of iron. Meantime I'll keep a sharp lookout here at the door."

But, in very truth, Tasso did not need much drawing. His prick was throbbing with desire. It was fairly burning to get into the folds of her soft recess. Yet he checked himself, in order to see what she would do.

21

She led him on until she backed against the inner seat. Then she sat down, and he remained standing before her. In this position his prick was now close to her face. She rubbed it softly between her hands, and then kissed its glowing head. She moved it over her nose and cheeks, sniffing up with delight the peculiar odour which exhaled from it.

Every time she brought it to her lips, Tasso pushed it gently against her mouth. Her lips gradually opened, and the prick seemed to pop in of its own accord. He felt her pliant tongue playing over its head, and twining round its indented neck. The sensation was so delicious that he could not help uttering a deep guttural "Ugh!" and pressing up against her.

She yielded to his pressure, and very soon he had her reclining on her back flat on the seat. Then bending over her he quickly drew up her nun's robes, and lifting her legs he pressed her thighs down on her body in such a way as to expose the whole of her beautiful bottom, and give him a full view of her delicious love chink, surrounded with luxuriant hair. Oh! How it seemed to pout out with a most unspeakable delight! He took his prick in his hand, and rubbed its glowing head between the soft moist lips.

This action proved just as pleasant to her as it

22

was delightful to him. She pushed upwards to meet him, and called too her friend:

"Look! Robina! There has been no failure, – he's just a-going to do it. Pity you could not come and watch it going in! Oh! It does feel nice! – Oh! So nice!"

"Ha! Ha! My dear," laughed Robina, "you will have to suffer a little before you know how really nice it is!"

Tasso now began to push in good earnest, and Lucia winced not a little as she felt the sharp pain, caused by the head of his huge prick forcing its way through the tight embrace of her vagina, for she was a true virgin, and her hymen had never been ruptured. However, she bore it bravely, especially as she knew her friend was watching.

"Robina," she called, to show her indifference to the pain, "I wish you would go behind and give him a shove, to make him push harder."

But just as she spoke, the obstructing hymen suddenly gave way, and his fine prick rushed up and filled all the inside of her cunt, and his hard balls flapped up against her bottom.

"Ah!" she cried, as she felt the inward rush of the vigorous tool. "Now it's all over! He's got it all in! – Well, it wasn't so bad after all. And now it feels delicious! – How nicely he makes it move in and out. – Can you see it, Robina?" she asked, as she noticed her friend stooping behind Tasso, and looking up between his legs.

"Yes, dear Lucia. I see your pretty slit sucking in his big tool, and I feel his two balls gathered up tightly in their bag. He certainly is no fool at this kind of work. I am sure he is just going to spurt his seed into you. – There! – Tell me, do you like it?"

"Oh! Yes! It feels grand! – He's shedding such a lot into me! And more is coming, too! It is the nicest thing I have ever felt!"

And throwing her arms about him she hugged him with all her might.

Presently he drew his prick out of her warm sheath. It was slightly tinged with blood, – the token of his victory and her pain. Robina carefully wiped it with her handkerchief, and coaxed him to sit down between them on the seat. Then they made signs to him to produce his slate.

Lucia wrote:

"Dear Tasso. I greatly enjoyed what you did to me. Have you any name for it, that I may know what to ask for when I want it again?"

He smiled when he read the question, and then wrote a reply.

"It is called fucking."

Then he handed her the slate.

"Doing this is called fucking," she said to Robina.

Then pointing to his prick, which was beginning to stand again, in all the pride of youthful vigour, she wrote:

"What is the name of this?"

"It is called a 'prick' and yours is a 'cunt'," he wrote, "and they are made for one another."

Lucia laughed when she read it.

"Why, Robina," she cried, "we are getting a grand lesson. His thing is a prick and our slits are cunts; but he need not have told us that they are made for one another, for all the world knows that. What a pity he can't talk! I would so much like to hear him speak of his prick and our cunts. But it is well that he can write about them."

Then she took the slate and wrote:

"Your prick is getting quite large and stiff again. Would you like to fuck Sister Robina?"

Tasso grinned.

"Do you know what I have just written?" said Lucia, turning to Robina. "I have asked him if he would like to fuck you?"

"Oh! You horrid girl!" retorted Robina. "Of course he will say he would. Men always love a change of cunts. I suppose we must use that word now when talking to each other."

Tasso's delight was almost insupportable. He longed to use his tongue, and give audible expression to his joy. But that would have spoiled everything. So he resolved to persevere with his role, and wrote:

"If Sister Robina will follow your kind example, and grant me the same favour, it will call forth the everlasting gratitude of poor dumb Tasso."

"Why, he has written quite a nice little speech, Robina," said Lucia, handing her the slate.

"He writes a fairly good hand, too," smilingly remarked Robina; and then handing back the slate, said, "Tell him to stand up, and let me kiss his prick as you did."

Lucia wrote accordingly:

"Stand up, Tasso, and let her kiss your prick first, and then you can fuck her cunt just as much as you like."

Tasso at once complied. He stood before Robina, and pushed between her knees so as to place his prick more conveniently for her eager inspection and caresses.

Taking it tenderly in her hands, she felt it all over, as if measuring its size and power to give pleasure. Then she turned her attention to the heavy bags which held his large stones, and pushed

26

her fingers back even as far as the aperture behind.

Tasso repaid the caresses she gave him by bending to one side, and thrusting his hand up between her warm thighs. He grasped the fat lips of her cunt, and rubbed the hot clitoris which jutted out between them. Then, as they both became eager for the sweet consummation to which these thrilling touches led, he gently pushed her back. She yielded readily enough, for her cunt was already moist with the expectation of taking in the delicious morsel she held in her hands. She allowed him to uncover all her hidden charms, and spread her thighs to their utmost extent. But just as she felt him inserting his fiery tool, she called to Lucia, who, though standing at the door, was intently watching Tasso's interesting operation.

"Dear Lucia, keep a strict watch! It would be an awful thing if anyone caught us here!"

"Don't be afraid," replied Lucia. "I'll keep a good lookout. There's no one about now, and I only take a peep now and then to see how you and Tasso are enjoying yourselves. I love to watch you. I was just thinking, that next to being fucked one's self, there is nothing like watching another going through it. I never saw your cunt look so well as it did just now, when Tasso opened the lips, and rubbed the head of his prick inside the rosy folds.

And now he has got it all in. It is most delightful to watch it slipping in and out. But how is it that he does not seem to hurt you as he did me? For I notice that he got in quite easily, and you kept hugging him closely all the time! – Oh! How nice it must have felt!"

And Lucia pressed her hands between her own legs, and jerked her bottom backwards and forwards.

"My! How you talk, Lucia! But anyway, keep a good lookout, and you may watch me between times. I don't mind your seeing how much we are enjoying ourselves. Poor Tasso can't hear me, or I would tell him how well pleased I am. I am sure the squeezing of my cunt is making him feel that already."

She breathes heavily, and heaves her bottom up convulsively to meet his rapid thrusts.

"You might put your hand on us now, Lucia, if you like. – He's just finishing. – Oh! It's grand!"

And all her muscles relaxed as she reclined back, and Tasso lay panting on her belly.

Lucia sat down by them, and leaned over Tasso, squeezing her thighs together, for she felt her own fount of pleasure in the flow.

After a moment's rest, Tasso got up, shook himself, and having arranged his clothes, wrote on his slate:

"Dear kind ladies: You have made poor dumb Tasso very happy. Let me now thank you and return to my work, lest any harm should happen."

He then bowed himself out, and disappeared among the laurels.

# CHAPTER III.

## HOW ROBINA ENJOYED IT

ON THE following day, to Tasso's great delight, the two young nuns again sat near him, though in a different part of the grounds.

The sight of him naturally made them think of their late pleasures, and they began to talk of how and when they might safely meet him again in the summer-house.

Having been now fairly launched on the sea of pleasure, they felt irresistibly impelled to go on. They knew that they were running a tremendous risk, but the temptation was so great that they were ready to brave all the consequences.

So, watching their opportunity, they told Tasso on his slate that, if possible, they would come out that evening during the half hour allowed the nuns for private devotion before the usual service. It was his time for quitting work, putting away his tools, and retiring for the night, and the garden was then generally empty.

Lucia then reminded her friend that she had promised to tell her how it was that she felt no smart or pain when Tasso pushed his prick into her cunt.

"My dear Lucia," began Robina, "I think I may tell you, now that we understand one another, and have shaken off our terror of the confessional. Before I came here, I had for my Confessor a priest with a great appearance of sanctity; but, as I found to my cost, it was only a cloak to hide his real nature. He was of a strong lustful temperament. Why, dear, he actually forced me in the room of the Mother Superior, where he heard my confession. I often think he had me there with an evil design which the Superior not only had connived at, but helped to carry out. And strange to say, my confessions furnished him with the occasion he desired.

"I had to confess what arose out of a curious circumstance, – something like your dream. It happened thus:

"The evening before making my first confession after joining the Sisterhood of M——, I obtained permission to take a solitary walk of meditation in a field belonging to the Convent. Feeling tired, I sat down by the boundary hedge to rest. I had my Manual with me, and oddly enough was reading that part of the preparation for confession where the sins against chastity are referred to, and we are directed to examine our own conscience, and are asked if we have looked at indecent pictures, or touched either ourselves or others immodestly, etc., when I heard the voices of a man and a woman on the other side of the hedge.

"As they came up, the man said: 'See! What a fine sheltered spot! – Just what we were looking for!'

"Then they sat down and settled themselves on the grass. From their talk, they must have at once commenced playing with each other's private parts. They used such terms as 'prick,' and 'cunt,' and 'fucking,' which were then new to me. But I was at no loss to understand their meaning, from their talk, and the manner in which the words were applied.

"The man said: 'Pull up your petticoats as high as you can, and open your legs, so as to give me a full view of your pretty brown-haired cunt! – That's a dear! Oh! How luscious it looks! So hot and so moist! So velvety inside!'

" 'I am glad you like it!' she replied. 'But don't keep it waiting too long! Put in your prick and fuck me!'

"I know it was a very wicked thing to do, to remain there, listening to all this, but my curiosity was so great that I could not tear myself away.

"I then heard sounds, as if they were struggling or working together, and then she spoke in a gasping voice.

" 'Oh! I feel it up – ever so far!' she said. 'Push! My darling! – Push!'

"And then I heard their bellies smack together.

" 'Oh! Oh!' she cried. 'Your dear prick is filling my cunt with the most unspeakable delight!'

"He panted loudly as she continued. 'Oh! My love! That is so nice!'

"I listened to this with breathless interest, and the effect upon myself was overpowering. Without thinking of what I was doing, I put my hand on my affair, and rubbed it until I obtained relief. And while I was so occupied, they departed.

"This touching and rubbing I later confessed to the priest, and then I had to tell him the occasion and the circumstances, and had to repeat every word which I heard used. But I objected to saying such names, on the score of decency. To this he replied that there was no such a thing as indecency in the confessional, for it was a holy place, and it imparted a holy character to everything that was said and done at that time. So he made me say 'prick,' over and over again, and then asked me what I supposed it was.

"I replied that it seemed to me to be the name for the private part of a man, and that the other word I had heard, 'cunt,' was the corresponding part of the woman, and that 'fucking' was the joining of them together, which Nature made us understand was a very pleasant thing.

"Then he made me describe the excitement I felt in my own cunt during the time I was engaged in listening to the man and woman who were fucking.

"And as if this were not enough, he told me he wanted to know exactly how I put my hand on my cunt, and to let him see me do it.

"This, however, I at first flatly refused to do. My obstinacy angered him; for his face, which had been very red before, now grew purple, and his eyes looked as if they were starting out of his head.

"He caught me roughly by the arm. – I was kneeling by his side, you know. – He shook me as he said:

" 'Daughter, you have not yet learned the first of all virtues, – obedience. Stand up!'

"I did so.

" 'Now lift up your skirts and place your hand just as you have been describing it to me!'

"I jerked out the word 'Never!' through my compressed lips.

"He arose from the chair in which he had been sitting, and pushed me violently towards a sofa at the side of the room. He forced me down upon this, and then began pulling up my clothes.

" 'How dare you!' I said, in a very angry voice. 'If you were ten times a priest, I would not suffer you to take such liberties with me! Let me up, or I will cry out!'

"At this very moment, the Mother Superior walked in and came up, looking exceedingly vexed.

" 'Sister Robina! How can you behave in this unseemly manner? I am very sorry to find that I have such a refractory nun under my charge. Don't you know that you must obey this holy Father in all things?'

" 'But I won't obey him,' I retorted, 'when he wants me to do something that I believe to be wrong.'

" 'There you make a mistake,' was her reply. 'You may be sure that what a priest in the confessional requires you to do is always necessary and right. And even though the thought may be disagreeable to you, yet you are bound to submit.'

"'I won't!' I declared.

"'You shall!' she retorted, catching me by the shoulders, and pushing me over.

"I struggled with her, while the priest at the same time held my legs with one of his strong hands, and pulled up my clothes with the other.

"Between them both, I was powerless, and began to cry as I said:

"'You are making me break my vows!'

"'Not in the least, you silly girl. Don't you know he is under a vow as well as you are? And two vows, like two negatives, nullify one another. You are each only prevented from going with others, and your submission will be a praise-worthy act, for it will afford both him and yourself a necessary relief. Come, now! Show us that you understand the matter aright. Open your thighs, and let him see all that you have there. Nature meant that to be used, and in this manner; and with my sanction you can do so without blame. I heard what you just confessed, and approve of your using all those terms when engaged here with the holy Father.'

"But her fine sophistry did not quiet me. I still opposed them in every way I could.

"By this time the priest had forcibly drawn up

my skirts, and all my thighs, belly and bottom were exposed before him. He had even lifted my legs as well, and as I kicked them in the air in my struggles to get free, he pinched my naked bottom in the most savage manner, maddening me with pain, and making me jerk about in a manner that added greatly to his delight. I saw that his eyes were fixed upon my cunt, which I felt opening at every bound. He kept my legs wide apart, but I still struggled so hard that he was not able to place his hands upon my slit.

"Vexed at what she termed my silly obstinacy, the Mother Superior reprimanded me severely.

" 'You stupid thing!' she exclaimed. 'Keep quiet. Let him look at that saucy impudent cunt of yours. He shall do anything with it that he likes! – Now, Father Angelo, take your prick and thrust it well in! – It will be a good punishment, and only serve her right. – But show it to her first, that she may get the full benefit of the sight before she feels your hard firm thrusts.'

" 'He at once complied; and, taking out his prick, he stood up close to me. It was the first man's prick I had ever seen, and it terrified me by its extreme length, and its huge red head. All at once, he pushed it towards my face.

" 'Oh! Fie!' I cried. 'Take the monstrous thing away. – It is horrible!'

"And I shut my eyes.

"But the Mother Superior and the priest only laughed at me.

" 'What a fool you are!' she exclaimed.

"And taking the prick in her hand, she rubbed it over my face, made it pass under my nose, and about my mouth. In vain I tried to turn from it. She always managed to keep the firm warm thing playing around my face, until it nearly set me wild. And yet not altogether with anger, for strange to say, though I certainly disliked the man, still the touch of his prick and its peculiar smell had an effect on me which I could not resist. I began to feel a kind of pleasure in having my cunt exposed to his view, and felt a thrill of delight run through my veins when he put his hand on my slit and caressed the lips and tickled the clitoris.

"Noticing this, the Mother Superior removed the charger, and addressing the priest, said:

" 'Now, Father, you may try her. She seems tired out, or perhaps, – and I hope it is so, – she is coming to a better mind.'

"Then she put her hand softly under my chin, turned up my mouth and kissed me.

" 'Come, Sister,' she said. 'Take my advice. Submit gracefully, and it will be all the better for you. Know then, that I am fully resolved that you shall not leave this room until you have been well fucked.'

"Father Angelo then drew me to the end of the sofa, until my bottom rested on the very edge. He then fixed himself between my thighs, and spreading open the lips of my cunt with his fingers, while he pressed the head of his big red tool firmly against the entrance.

"Madame knelt on the floor beside us, and tucking up my clothes as high as she could, watched the operation.

"He pushed gently at first, then harder and harder, and hurt me considerably. I moaned with the pain, but I did not resist, for I now saw it was of no use, and I began to be on fire, and wish his tool was safely lodged inside.

"The Mother Superior now leaned over me and opening my bodice, drew up my breasts, and caressed the exposed bubbies with her hands.

"Then turning to him, she said, 'Can't you get in? Is it too tight? – Just wet her cunt and your prick, and you will find it easier.'

"He took away his prick, and in a moment I felt his tongue moving around the inside of my cunt, his lips sucking my clitoris.

"This had a strangely soothing and most delightful effect, and I smiled with pleasure.

" 'Ah! – You like that!' she said. 'You like to have your cunt licked and your clitoris sucked, do you? Well, you won't have the full pleasure until he gets his prick in, and drives it all the way up.'

"Meanwhile the priest was moistening his prick with spittle, and again placed it between the lips of my anxious slit. This time I did not shrink from his attack at all, but spread my thighs as widely apart as I could.

" 'Now, Father, push,' she cried; and putting her hand down, she grasped and squeezed my clitoris.

"I could feel the great hard head forcing its way in. You know now, Lucia, what a strange sensation of mingled pain and pleasure a woman experiences the first time a man's prick is driven into her cunt–"

"Shall I ever forget?" responded Lucia, with animation. "But in my case, the pain was only for a moment, for soon it was completely overbalanced by the pleasure."

"Yes; so I was glad to see," responded Robina. "But Tasso's prick is not by any means as thick as that of Father Angelo."

Poor Tasso's jaw fell a little as he listened to this confession.

"And somehow," she continued, "he uses his in a more gentle and coaxing way."

40

"So he does!" assented Lucia. "And Oh! Robina! I am longing so for it now. – But go on. Tell me how they finished the job, and how you liked it."

"Well," resumed Robina, "the touch of Madame's fingers excited me greatly, and I met the next push he gave with an upward heave. I at once felt something give way inside, and the hot stiff prick glided up into my cunt and filled the whole cavity with such a sensation of voluptuous delight as I had never experienced before in my life. The Mother Superior kissed me again; and she squeezed the lips of my cunt around his prick as she asked me this question:

" 'Now, Robina, how do you like that? – Could there be anything nicer than the feel of a man's prick stirring that way in your cunt? May he fuck you when he wishes hereafter?'

" 'Oh! Oh! It's delicious! – Yes! He may fuck me as much as he likes,' I could not help adding, as I felt the great prick moving swiftly in and out. 'Oh! Oh! That is so – so – nice!'

"Madame seemed well pleased at her success. Nothing gave her so much pleasure, I afterwards learned, as seeing a woman fucked for the first

41

time; and in the pursuit of this form of pleasure, she had had every one of her nuns fucked by one or another of the priests who acted as Confessors."

"I am sure," said Lucia, "that it is very pleasant to stand by and watch another woman being fucked. I know I liked to look at you while Tasso was fucking you. I dearly love to watch a prick working in and out between the hairy lips of your cunt. But go on, – tell me more."

"The Mother Superior asked me," Robina continued, "if I enjoyed the feel of her hand about my cunt while it was being fucked.

"'It greatly increases the pleasure,' I replied.

"'I expected it would,' she said. 'And now let me put your hands on mine, and perhaps that will not only add still more to your enjoyment, but also give me a little taste of the pleasure, as well.'

"Speaking thus, she drew up her clothes, and placed my hand between her thighs. I pushed it up until I met an immense pair of thick hairy lips, and, diving my fingers into the chink between I felt a cunt overflowing with moisture, and burning with heat.

"I rubbed my hand in and out of this crevice, – an operation which she informed me was called 'frigging,' – keeping time to the quick prods of Father Angelo's prick in my own cunt, while she kept pushing her bottom backwards and forwards.

"'That's a darling!' she said, with convulsive starts. 'Oh! Now it's coming! – Fuck! Father! Fuck! – Push your stones hard against her arse! – Drive your fingers into my cunt, Robina, – not one but two – three – four! – All you can! – Oh!!'

"And she squeezed the lips of my cunt so hard that I almost screamed out, while the Father actually bellowed with delight as he poured a flood of hot sperm into my throbbing recess.

"Madame finished up by leaning over me, rubbing her bare bubbies on mine, and darting her luscious tongue into my open mouth."

"Ah! Robina!" sighed Lucia. "That was a fuck! Your charming account of it has set me wild! My cunt is just burning!" – And pulling up her skirt in front, she continued, "Look at it, darling! – Tasso is watching, too, but I don't mind. – I would give all the world for a good fuck now! – Put your hand on it and frig me, darling, and let Tasso see you."

"Lucia! Are you mad?" chided Robina. "How

fortunate that the Sisters have gone in! – But we must not delay now. And see! Tasso is showing us his prick! Watch him, frigging it with his hands."

"Yes. Robina. Tasso is a dear fellow! How well he understands what to do! – Oh! How nice his prick looks! How stiffly it stands up! Wouldn't I like to have it in my cunt now? I love to watch it while you are rubbing me there! – Oh! How nice! Now faster! – Push your finges up! – Oh!! There!!! – Now let me rest, and I will go with you in a moment."

And with a sigh she leaned her head on Robina's shoulder.

Tasso was now in great need of relief himself. He felt his balls nearly bursting with their contained charge. Satisfying himself that there was no one in the garden but themselves, he stepped nimbly up to them, his fine prick standing out before him, and boldly pushed it up close to Robina's face. She put her hand upon it, and knowing well what he wanted, drew it to her mouth. Then she placed her other hand on his balls, which were also exposed. The soft touch of her fingers on those highly sensitive organs thrilled him with delight. He thrust forward his prick, and pressed its head against her lips. They opened, and in popped the prick, and she began to suck.

He gently worked his arse backwards and forwards, and thus fucked her mouth, as if it were a cunt. She held his balls firmly, and tightened her grasp around the roots of his prick. Her pliant tongue wound around its head, while she sucked with all her force.

Then came the gushing seed, which filled her mouth even to overflowing. She held all she could until he withdrew his prick, and then ejected the slimy sperm on the grass.

Tasso smiled his thanks, and at once turned away, but they detained him long enough to make an appointment with him for the evening. With a bow he left them, after which they also speedily retired.

# CHAPTER IV.

## OTHER NUNS DESIRE IT

THE two young nuns succeeded in having a pleasant meeting with Tasso not only on that evening, but on some days following. And by watching their opportunity, they several times enjoyed with him their favourite sport.

As they had done their utmost to avoid attracting observation, they thought that their friendly intercourse with Tasso had escaped the notice of everyone. But as is usually the case in such matters, they were very much mistaken.

The Sisters were not permitted to form special friendships; yet when they enjoyed any freedom together, they naturally fell into pairs or sets.

There were two other nuns, named Aminda and Pampinea, who had similar tastes and usually walked together.

They observed the intimacy which had sprung up between the Sisters Lucia and Robina, and the gardener; and feeling certain that there was something in the wind, they watched him closely.

So it was arranged that Pampinea was to hide among the thick bushes by the side of the summerhouse one evening, to watch and report to her friend all that she could find out.

At their next meeting, Aminda at once asked:

"Well, Pampinea, dear, what news have you?"

"Most wonderful, – beyond our wildest imagination. Frightful in one sense, delightful in another. I must begin at the very beginning."

"Yes; do, dear."


"I found a capital hiding place, where I was quite concealed, and yet, by drawing aside a branch I could see right into the summer-house. Shortly afterwards, the two Sisters, looking as innocent as a pair of doves, came and sat down. And as soon as all the others had left the garden, Tasso marched in with a broad grin upon his face. They smiled on him, and let him place them as he liked. So without losing a moment, he had them both kneeling on the seat with their ends turned out. Then he whipped up their petticoats and uncovered to view their large white bottoms.

"Then, my dear, he took out his big red 'what-you-call-it.'

"I was horrified at first, and felt ready to sink into the ground with shame, but it is odd how soon one gets accustomed to these things!

"I could not keep my eyes off it. I wondered at its size, and its great red head. Well, my dear, he pushed it up against the bottom first of the one, and then of the other.

"They had no feeling of modesty, at all, for they poked themselves out, and spread their legs apart so as to let him see all they had, – their cute little bottom-holes, hairy slits, and everything.

"He smacked their bottoms with his tool, and then pushed it all into Lucia's slit. She seemed to like it well, for she laughed as she felt it going up. But she did not hold it long, for he quickly pulled it out and shoved it into Robina in the same way.

"Then when he had given her a similar prod, he went back to Lucia, and so on from one to the other.

"All the time they were thus engaged, they continued laughing and talking to one another; and, my dear, you would hardly credit the words they used. They said that Tasso had fucked them that way before, but they thought it very pleasant. They liked to feel his hairy belly rubbing against their bottoms and that his prick seemed to get even further into their cunts than ever before. – Tell me, did you ever hear such words?"

"I did. I remember hearing them when I was a girl at school. They are coarse words, and perhaps for that very reason all the more exciting. So go on, and use them as much as you please. Your description is very amusing, – and, do you know, it is causing me a peculiarly pleasant feeling in my cunt? You see I use them, too. – Would you mind putting your hand on it, dear, while you are describing what followed?"

"Not in the least. I shall quite enjoy it, and you can do the same for me, for my cunt too is burning with heat. And I have had to pet it. Twice I witnessed the wonderful enjoyment which both Lucia and Robina showed, when they had Tasso's prick poking their cunts."

Then the two nuns, in very un-nun like fashion, managed to get their hands on the other's cunt as Pampinea went on:

"After changing several times, I noticed that Tasso's prick looked larger and redder each time it came out. He plunged it with great force into Sister

Lucia; his belly smacked aginst her bottom. He remained as if glued to her behind, but Robina stood up, and pushing her hands between them, began 'fiddling with his stones and Lucia's arse,' as she called it.

"After a couple of minutes or so he drew out his prick, now all soft and hanging down, and some kind of white stuff dripping from it. Lucia then turned about and sat down, and made Tasso sit on the seat beside her, while Robina knelt on the ground before them, between Tasso's legs.

"Lucia put her hand on his balls and Robina took hold of his prick. And, my dear, she put it into her mouth, wet as it was.

"Lucia laughed: 'Ah! Robina, you are like me, – I love to taste the flavour of your cunt, and now I hope you won't find that the flavour of mine is disagreeable.'

"Robina lifted her head, and said: 'Not in the least. I like the salty taste, and the smell is delicious.'

"Then she recommenced her sucking, while Lucia's fingers played about the root of the prick, and occasionally touched the chin and sucking lips of her friend.

"Tasso's prick grew stronger, until its head seemed too large for Robina's mouth to take it all in.

Lucia remarked its size and said: 'I think, Robina, that you have sucked Tasso's prick into working order again. What would you think of getting him to lie down there on his back, and then for you to straddle over him, place his prick in your cunt with your own hand? – And I will help you if you like? Then go through the motions yourself and make him suck you at your leisure.'

"'Capital notion! Let us at once put it into execution, for our time is nearly up.'

"They both stood up and soon had Tasso on his back on the ground. Then Robina, tucking up her skirts all around, straddled over him and made her cunt descend upon his standing prick.

"Lucia fixed it aright, and kept it steady as a candlestick with her hand, while Robina, with a downward push caused it to rush up into her to the very hilt.

"Lucia then laid herself down by Tasso's side and rested her cheek on his belly, so close to his prick that she was able to touch with her tongue at the same time both the little fleshy knot of Robina's cunt, and the prick as often as it was pressed down, while she allayed her own excitement by working a finger between the hairy lips of her own affair.

"Altogether it was a most voluptuous scene.

51

What, between their lustful motions, their wanton cries, and the sweet visible union of prick and cunt, nothing could be more exciting. I envied them with all my heart, and I am sure, Aminda, you would have done so too."

"I am quite certain I should, – and more. I know of no reason why we may not share in their sports – do you? But we must go, now. We will talk the matter over on the next opportunity."

# CHAPTER V.

## LUCIA GETS MORE OF IT

WE MUST now return to the two young nuns first mentioned in this narrative.

The day had come for Lucia to complete her confession to Father Joachim in the private room of the Mother Abbess. She and Robina had pledged one another, as you will doubtless remember, not to refer in any way during confession to their intercourse with Tasso, – but they agreed later that they might safely tell the priest how Lucia had seen his prick, and how they had talked together and petted each other's cunts.

Let us pass on then to the scene.

Lucia is kneeling beside the priest, who is seated on a comfortable arm-chair in Madame's private apartments. This little room is elegantly fitted up as a lady's boudoir. It had two doors, one opening into her reception room, – the other partially concealed, led by a secret passage to the Sacristy of the Convent Chapel. And by this way, the priests who officiated there could always visit the Mother Abbess without being noticed.

What a handsome man is Father Joachim! The bloom of youth is still upon his cheek. His white untarnished skin and full red lips had made many a voluptuously-inclined maid sigh with unrequited desire. Though somewhat of a tendency to embonpoint, yet his body might be termed a veritable cushion, in which a thousand dimples hid themselves until at the proper moment they were called into action. The fame of this handsome priest had travelled before him. For his celebrated amour with an angel was a stock story in monastries and convents. Robina and Lucia were not unacquainted with it, the Mother Abbess having retailed the gossip previous to Father Joachim's coming.

Lucia has just reached that part of her confession where she tells the priest how, having occasion to go to the Little-house, she saw through the perforated door, the gardener Tasso, coming up, unbuttoning his trousers, and taking out his tool and making water.

"Do you remember my daughter, the name

you mentioned in your last confession for a man's tool? I wish you to use it now."

"Well, Father, if you will have me use these naughty words, it was his prick that I saw."

The priest's eyes now began to glisten, and there was a slight tremor in his hand as he said:

"Yes; it makes your confession more real and exact. Now tell me precisely all he did."

Lucia could hardly repress a smile, for she felt that she now had the priest in leading strings, and she was determined to draw him on. So she spoke out more boldly as she continued:

"When he took out his prick, he held it in his hand and shot forth his water straight before him, and he looked down on his prick while he piddled. When he finished, he shook it two or three times. Then he drew the skin back from its red head, which made it grow larger and stick out more stiffly before him."

"Now tell me, my daughter, exactly and fully what effect the view of Tasso's prick had upon yourself, and use the terms you have already uttered in confession."

"Oh! Father! How can I tell you such things?" And she leaned her elbow on his knee.

"It is quite necessary, my child, and the more particular you are in every word and in every detail the better your confession will be."

"Well, Father, I suppose I must tell you everything. – As I kept looking at the prick, I felt a warm glow all between my legs, and my cunt began to itch so terribly that I pulled up my petticoats and squeezed it with my hand. Then I pushed my finger in and rubbed the inside as hard as I could."

"Were you standing up at the time?"

"I was, Father."

"Were your legs separated?"

"They were, Father."

"Now get up, separate your legs, and stand just as you did at the time."

Lucia stood up and straddled her legs.

"I am glad to find you so true a daughter of our Holy Mother Church, – for obedience to your spiritual guides is the very essence of her teaching.

"Now put your hand on your cunt just as you did when you were looking at the gardener's prick."

Lucia lifted her clothes at one side and put her hand on her cunt. The priest looked greatly excited, and said:

"But, my daughter, I want to see it."

"Well, Father you must raise my clothes yourself."

The priest's cheeks flamed with amorous desire; and the fire of lust flamed in his eyes as he lifted her petticoats in front, and stooping forward, he was enabled to gaze upon the revealed beauties of her charming cunt. Then with a quick motion of his other hand, he rapidly unbuttoned his breeches as he said:

"Now, my daughter, that the scene may be complete, I want you to look at my prick while you are rubbing your cunt. You know these things are no sin with a holy man like me. See! Here is my prick! Look at it!"

And placing his hand behind on her naked bottom, he drew her in towards him.

The priest's burly prick, still larger and stronger than Tasso's, stood up boldly before her.

"Does the sight of this prick excite you in the same way that the gardener's did?"

"Oh! It does, Father. But are you sure it is not wrong to look at it?"

"Quite sure, my daughter, and you may put your hand on it too, without fear of sin. My child, your confidence is most refreshing. Yes, I would like you to feel it all over, – and the balls too, if you will, while I explore your delicious cunt."

Then he pushed his finger up and began to rub it quickly in and out.

"Good! My child, now come over and rest upon this lounge."

With his arm round her, he drew her to the end

of the couch, laid her on her back, lifted her legs, and pushed her petticoats above her navel. He then stooped over her and with his hand directed his prick between the moist lips of her itching cunt.

As soon as she felt it in that sensitive recess, she panted out:

"Oh! Father! What do you want to do?"

"To push my prick into your cunt and fuck you. Isn't that the right word to use? May I fuck you?"

"Why, Father, you told me I must obey you in everything, and if you want to fuck me, of course I must let you."

The priest smiled approval, and gave a lunge with his prick.

"Oh! It's going in! – Oh! Father! – How strong your prick is! I feel it up to the very centre of my belly! – Oh! Do you like fucking me?"

"Yes, my daughter. Your cunt holds my prick deliciously. I have fucked many of the Sisters, but I like your cunt best of all. And especially because you talk so freely. – Now, heave your arse! – That's the way! – Now! – Oh! – It's just coming! – Put your arms around me! – Hug me! Tighter yet! Now tell me how you feel."

"Dear Father, your prick in my cunt feels lovely – I would like to keep it there forever! Fuck! Fuck! Fuck!"

The priest drove his prick up with his full force. His brawny loins smacked against the soft cheeks of her arse, and his hard balls pressed against the sensitive edges of her bottom-hole, while the flood of his fierce passion filled the recesses of her well satisfied and delighted cunt.

"Dear, dear Father!" she cries in her ecstasy. "Give me your lips to lick! – Oh! Blessed Virgin! I feel your lovely prick emptying itself inside of me! – Now I come! I come – There! There! – Oh! God! What pleasure!"

"Yes! Darling daughter! Suck my mouth!" shouts the delighted priest.

Then no sound is heard except the sucking of lips and the pleasing noise made by the priest's prick as it gurgles in and out of Lucia's cunt. His prick still remained stiff, though he had spent freely. This was too much for the partly distracted Lucia. She lost control of her senses, in fact, fairly swooned away.

# CHAPTER VI.

## THE MOTHER ABBESS DELIGHTS IN IT

WHEN she regained her senses, she looked about. The priest was gone. There was a feeling as if something were rubbing and titillating her grotto of love, and she opened her eyes wide. To her intense surprise she saw that the Mother Abbess was bending over her and she felt her fingers were playing with her dripping cunt.

"My daughter," she said, "you have behaved well. I am glad you showed such child-like obedience, and put your body to the holy service of giving relief to that worthy priest. It is no sin with him, you know, nor with me either. And I greatly commend your good sense in using all those terms which so increase and intensify these precious delights. And whenever you are with me, on similar occasions, I wish you always to use such words.

I saw you fucked, my child. I was close by, when Father Joachim's prick was prodding your cunt, and I heard everything you said. Now open your legs wide. I want to kiss your cunt while it is still wet with his holy seed."

Lucia lay as if thunderstruck. She did not know what to say in reply, but she willingly spread her legs as she felt the warm breath of the Mother Abbess blowing aside the hairs of her cunt. Then she felt her soft tongue licking all round the inside of the slit, and then the whole of the clitoris drawn into her mouth. This was very enjoyable, but when she felt her tongue actually penetrating the passage, she could not resist putting down her hand, and laying it gently on the head of the Mother Abbess as she said:

"Dear Mother, how good you are! You are making my cunt glow with as much pleasure as when the Holy Father was fucking me."

The only response of the Mother Abbess was to work her tongue more nimbly in and out, and to push a moistened finger into her bottom-hole.

This last act caused a new sensation to Lucia, and made her press up against the mouth of the Mother Abbess and cry:

"Oh! My! That's so nice! Dear Mother, I am just going to spend! – My cunt and bottom are all in a glow! – Oh! Oh! – There! It's coming!"

And the Mother Abbess skilfully frigged her arse, while she lapped up with her tongue every drop of the love juice which exuded from Lucia's hot little recess.

The Mother Abbess allowed her to rest for a while, then kissed her, and said:

"I am very glad you have had so much enjoyment. Will you not do the same for me?"

"That I will, dear Mother. I am indeed longing to see and pet your dear cunt, only I was afraid to ask you."

And Lucia stood up, as the Mother Abbess took her place.

"See then, here it is!"

And laying herself back the Mother Abbess drew up her petticoats and spread her legs wide apart.

Lucia had never before seen such a cunt as that which was now opened to her view. – So large, so hairy! Such immense lips! The thick fleshy clitoris stuck out like a boy's cock! And the red chink below it was deep and bathed in moisture.

She was of course familiar with her own little chink, which was young and fresh, and had a pert and innocent air about it. And she had often seen and closely examined Sister Robina's cunt, which was fuller and more open, and had a strong lust-provoking look about it, – but even Robina's was small and poor in comparison with the great shaggy affair of the Mother Abbess. From being long in the habit of affording relief to all these burly priests, its naturally thick lips had become enormously developed, and its capacity for taking in pricks of any dimensions was unlimited. Evidently nothing could startle this woman. In fact, she never saw a jackass with his tool extended, or viewed a stallion's telescopic tickler without wishing that she had it packed in her capacious hot-box.

Such was the cunt which Lucia now stooped over. She drew open the great fat lips, and as she looked into the deep rosy chink, she thought:

"Oh! That I had a man's prick, that I might plunge into these soft folds!"

But not having the prick, she could only do what little a woman could. So she placed her mouth in the open chink, sucked the clitoris with a will, and when she had forced an emission, she began to lick up the flowing juice.

She was however, suddenly interrupted. A man's hand pushed under her chin, and gently raised her head. Looking up with surprise, she saw another of the holy Fathers, named Ambrose, standing by her side, and his prick, still larger than Father Joachim's poking against her face.

In reply to her astonished look, he said:

"Let me, my child. This is what she wants. Pleasant as no doubt your mouth and tongue are, there is nothing like the real man's prick itself. Good Mother, may I take this sweet daughter's place? If you will permit, I am ready to serve you, and she can play with my prick and balls whilst I give full satisfaction to your heated and longing cunt."

"You are very welcome, Father Ambrose. I did not expect you for another full hour yet. Give me a satisfactory poke first, and by the time you are ready again, Sister Lucia will, I am sure, gladly avail herself of the services of your noble tool."

Without delay, Father Ambrose knelt close up to her great fat rump, now flattened out on the edge of the couch.

With one fierce, rapid thrust, he buried his enormous tool in her open cunt, while she, giving the fullest swing to her randy amorous inclinations, called out.

"Now Lucia, hold his prick by the roots. Keep a firm grip on his bollocks, – his balls, you know, –

and pinch his arse well. That's the way to make him fuck with life and spirit."

At each of these smutty words, the priest made a fresh plunge, and she as eagerly bounded to meet him.

Lucia gladly obeyed her Superior, and with a merry laugh pushed one hand between the Mother Abbess and the priest's hairy belly, and compressed her fingers as tightly as she could round the root of his prick. The other hand she put behind and took hold of the priest's cods, – first one and then the other, for they were too big for her hand to contain them both at once.

The holy Father now checked his speed, and, wishing to prolong the sweet joy, worked deliberately with a long steady stroke, pulling out the whole of his prick except the tip each time he drew back; while the Mother Abbess, more eager in her lust, crossed her feet over his back, and clung to him with arms and legs. But Lucia got so excited from watching his prick as it rushed in and out between the large clinging lips of Madame's voluptuous cunt, that she threw off all reserve, and pulled up her clothes and rubbed her naked cunt and belly against the firm cheeks of the priest's muscular backside. Then embracing him tightly round the loins with her arms, she joined in every push, tickling his arse most delightfully with the hair of her cunt.

This quickly brought on the climax, and the priest, with a loud exclamation of delight deluged the cunt of the Mother Abbess with his flowing sperm.

They rested a little, but with the secret parts of the bodies fully exposed, ready for either viewing or petting as might be desired.

Then the Mother Abbess produced some choice wine and spiced cakes. Each glass of wine which the good priest drank, he first seasoned by rubbing it on the cunt of one or the other, while they in like manner rubbed their glasses on his prick.

The Mother Abbess wanted them to hurry, and told Lucia to suck his prick to get him into fucking order.

Then the Father sat up, pointed to his prick and said:

"See how the fellow stands now!"

Then he cried:

"I want to fuck your cunt, Lucia! Let me see it! – It is just right! – Now kneel here on the edge of this lounge. Lift up your arse as high as you can. And will you, good Mother, put it in for me, and while I am fucking, play with us any way you like?"

The Mother Abbess knew what was implied in that permission, and at once began to finger both their bottoms.

The priest, however, did not get in as speedily as he expected. Lucia had not as yet taken in a prick of such abnormal proportions as that of Father Ambrose, and it stuck fast in the entrance of her cunt.

"Oh!" he cried. "This is grand! Her cunt is so tight that it won't let my prick in! But I like it all the more! – Does my prick hurt you, my daughter?"

"It does a little, Father. But I can bear it. – Ha! Oh! – Go softly! – Now push again! – I am trying to open my cunt for you. – There! It's getting in! Oh! Now I feel it going up! – up! – Oh! How immense it seems! I can feel it up to my very heart! My cunt is quite filled with it! Ah! Now it goes in easily enough! – Oh! Oh! That's delicious! Fuck me, Father! Fuck me! – More! More!"

She dwelt upon the word with such a libidinous accent as nearly set the priest wild, and caused him to drive his prick so forcibly in and out of her thrilling cunt as made the couch and everything movable near them vibrate with the violence of his powerful strokes.

In the meantime the Mother Abbess had worked

her passions up to an almost ungovernable pitch. She was visibly spending. In her frenzy of voluptuousness she almost tore their bottoms with her nails, as she urged on their mad ecstasy until Lucia's rolling eyes and heaving bottom told of the exquisite pleasure she was experiencing. Even the priest's eyes glittered and flashed, and his whole form quivered as he poured into Lucia's womb a flood of love's soothing-syrup.

"Ha! My pretty nun! What think you now?" shouts the Mother Abbess, apparently crazed with lust. "Do you know of another joy equal to this?"

With these words she secured possession of a rod and proceeded to lay it on the bounding arses of both priest and nun.

"Nice, plump arse!" she cries, lashing Lucia's posteriors severely. "Take that! And that! – So! – That makes you bounce, eh? – Now, Father, it is your turn."

So saying she cut the priest across the big fat cheeks of his arse so severely that he bounded like a rubber ball.

Lucia madly digs her fingers into its cheeks and holds the priest in such a firm grip that he cannot move. The Mother Abbess next gives Lucia a turn with the rod. Though the blows are quick and heavy, the girl is unmindful of them. She utters a loud shriek indicative of ecstatic pleasure. The priest expresses his blissful feelings in a pleased grunt. The Mother Abbess lays aside the rod, and then they all sank down, clutched in each other's arms.

# CHAPTER VII.

## IT IS THE CAUSE OF A MIRACLE

MEANWHILE, our friends Pampinea and Aminda held a consultation as to the best means of securing a share of Tasso's much prized services. Of course they neither felt nor acted as ordinary women. From the forced constraint under which they lived, their passions when aroused were almost uncontrollable; and the fact of Tasso's being unable, as they supposed, to either hear or speak, induced them to regard him as more of a machine than a man, and treat him so.

It was therefore agreed that Pampinea, the bolder of the two, was to write on his slate that she had seen all that he had done to the two Sisters in the Summer-house, and to invite him to go with them and do the same.

So waiting their opportunity, Pampinea went up and held out her hand for the slate. He gave it readily.

But what was she to write? After several abortive attempts she produced the following:

"I saw you in the Summer-house with the Sisters Lucia and Robina. I saw what you were doing. It seemed to please them so much that Sister Aminda and I would like you to teach us the same delightful game. – You may trust us, we will not tell any one, – no, not even confess it to the priest."

When he read it, he looked up with an amused but very pleased expression. Pampinea smiled in return, and pointed to the Summer-house. He nodded, and motioned to her to enter it.

The two Sisters looked carefully around; and, seeing no one about, sauntered up to the place, entered, and sat down.

Tasso quickly followed them. He assumed a half-witted expression as he stood before Pampinea, scratching his head, and at the same time making the huge bulkiness of his swelling prick as prominent as he could.

With an inquiring glance, she pointed to it as if asking what it was.

Oh! How his eyes did twinkle as he took her hand and rubbed it over his tool, letting her feel how it bounded and reared in its confinement. Her fingers began to fumble with the opening of his

71

trousers. He undid the buttons, and with a dexterous movement brought the whole length of that stately machine into view.

The Sisters started! They had never seen a man's prick displayed openly before them in that fashion. It is true that Pampinea indeed, had seen it before, but then it was in the dusk of the evening, and was always popping out of one cunt and into the other, and she remembered that when he had finally drawn it out, it had an exhausted, shrunken and crest-fallen appearance. But now it stood erect, in all the power, and all the freshness, and all the beauty of its youthful vigour.

Their eyes devoured it. Their hungry little mouths of cunts began to water for it. They felt their quims throb with the first impulses of pleasure. They were quite ready even now, to fall on their backs, spread apart their legs, and allow him to fondle and view and pet their sweet treasures. They longed for that blissful moment when he should part their jutting lips, and then put in his dear prick and let it revel in the sweets within. Still, with womanly instinct they held back and let him make the first move, and select whichever of them he might choose to commence with.

He did not long leave them in doubt.

There was a bold dash about Pampinea which strongly attracted him. Men always admire courage in a woman, especially when it tends to confidence in themselves; and she had shown a freedom from fear, with respect to him, which was simply delightful.

Like an Eastern devotee he dropped on his knees before her, and with his hands reverently raised the coarse garment of the nun as if it were a costly veil which sheltered the object of his worship.

Having gone so far, Pampinea was not the woman to halt now. She therefore allowed him to proceed, and to act according to the instincts of his nature.

She suffered him to open her thighs, to draw her to the edge of the seat, and push her back. Then, when she felt his fingers amorously examining and probing her cunt, feeling its moist creases and soft folds, and was also conscious that his bold eyes were running over all the beauties of these secret parts, so blushed a rosy blush of pleasure from head to foot, and felt a thrill of delight pervade the regions of love, until the very lips of her cunt seemed to part in a gentle smile with the anticipation of the approaching joys.

Aminda looked on with great interest, trying to imagine how she would feel herself under similar circumstances, when she suddenly remembered that Tasso could neither speak nor hear, and so she said,

"Dear Sister, don't you feel terribly ashamed at his looking at you there?"

"Not at all, dear," replied Pampinea. "Strange to say, I don't mind it in the least. I really like it now, – it seems so natural."

"Well," said Aminda, "it may be quite natural; but at first – well, at all events – it does look very queer. Anyhow, I feel that I would love to watch what he is doing to you forever. You don't dislike it, Pampinea, do you, dear?"

"No. I like you to watch. – Oh! Now I feel him rubbing against me that part which Lucia called his prick, and I can't tell you, dear, how nice it feels! He's trying to get it in now! – Oh! It's hurting me a little. But the pleasure is just maddening. Oh! Aminda! He's just got it in! – Now the pain is over, and he has pushed it all up, it feels delightful! – I cannot tell you how delicious it is, now that he is moving it in and out! Can you see it, dear?"

"Oh! Yes! – I see it plainly enough! – How easily it slips in and out! – It must indeed feel very nice! My own cunt, – at least that's what Lucia and Robina called theirs–"

"Well! – What about your cunt, my dear?"

"Oh! My cunt is tingling all over at the sight! – I do hope Tasso will like mine as he likes yours. Oh! How delicious it must feel to be fucked! – Isn't that the word?"

"Yes! – Oh! I can't talk now. – Fucking is delightful. – No terms – can – express – how – delicious – it feels!"

These words were uttered in successive jerks as Tasso drove in and out his red and swollen tool, while the hungry lips of her quivering cunt sucked it in with all the eagerness of the highest and voluptuous enjoyment.

Aminda shared their transports, and putting her hand on her own itching slit, forced her finger for the first time up the thrilling passage of her cunt.

"Tell me now, Pampinea, how do you feel?" cried Aminda, vigorously working her excited cunt.

"I – I – Oh! You heavenly man! – I must move my backside, too! – Don't ask me, Aminda! It's just too sweet to talk about! – Oh! I am all wet inside of me! – But you won't take it out, will you?" she pleadingly asks of Tasso, forgetful of his being powerless to hear.

"His prick is covered with oil," remarked Aminda. "I guess he must be nearly done. – At least I hope so," she adds, in a slightly petulant tone.

Tasso was now fucking the long-deprived maid

with all his strength. His finely developed prick was as stiff as ever; and every time he thrust it in to the full, Pampinea uttered little shrieks of delight. At last he made a quick thrust, and buried his prick in the anxious and longing cunt to its fullest extent, and then ceased his motions.

"Oh! Aminda!" cried Pampinea. "He is squirting hot streams into me! – Oh! Oh! There he goes again! Oh! I can not tell you of the sweet, sweet feeling that is within me. I only wish he would not take it out! I want it right over again!"

"That is indeed unkind of you, Pampinea," said Aminda, poutingly. "You know I have been fingering my cunt until I am almost mad with desire. Come, now! Do let me have a taste of what you have just felt."

While she was speaking these words, Tasso withdrew himself from Pampinea's luscious cunt. The fact was, all this fucking was beginning to tell a littleupon the gardener's vitality. Yet such was the tempting nature of the feast which was being constantly spread before him that, to save his soul, he could not resist the offerings.

Pampinea was wildly excited by the workings of Tasso's prick. She still imagined that something was working within her, for after Tasso had taken his prick from her, she continued the motions just as though she were again being fucked.

The gardener now turned his attention to Aminda, who was eagerly awaiting her turn. She certainly was a very beautiful woman, and as fresh and sweet as a full blown rose. The red blood mantled her cheek; her lily white skin was without flaw. Her eyes were aflame with passion. Her position was such as to expose her most secret charms, the sight of which instantly made Tasso's prick arise once more.

"Do you like to look at my cunt?" inquired Aminda artlessly upon the slate.

Tasso nods his head vigorously.

"I love to look at your prick," she again writes.

This breathing spell gave Tasso a splendid opportunity to raise a stiff prick. He knew that he had spent heavily in Pampinea, and the result would be that his staff when it once hardened again, would remain stiff for quite a period. As he saw his prick become as hard as a stone, he could not contain himself any longer. The sight of Aminda's pouting little love-nest added to his joy.

Then he fell upon his knees between the plump white thighs, and exclaimed:

"Oh! Mother of God! What a glorious feast!"

As he spoke each word, he greedily kissed Aminda's quivering cunt.

"He speaks! He speaks!" cries Pampinea, awakened to herself at the sound of Tasso's voice.

But the gardener paid no attention to her. He saw only Aminda and her secret beauties. He opens the lips of her anxious cunt, and pushes his big stiff prick right into her without heeding either her cries or her protestations.

The girl's cries however, were not unheard by others. The Mother Abbess and Father Joachim, who were indulging in a little stroll through the grounds, were attracted to the Summer-house by such unseemly noises.

And what a sight it was that greeted their eyes!

There was Pampinea, lying upon the ground, with disordered attire, and vigorously rubbing the clitoris and stiffened inner lips of her still slippery cunnie, while not far from her, Tasso and Aminda were battling right royally in amorous warfare.

"By the Great God above!" shouts the intoxicated Tasso. "That was a fine return! – Ha! Ha! There is another for thee! Now, Now! My beautiful angel, give it back right quickly!"

"A miracle! A miracle!" shouts the Mother Abbess. "The dumb speak, and the deaf hear! Bear witness to this wondrous thing, Father Joachim!"

"Aye! Aye!" returns Father Joachim. "This must go upon the records. It will be recorded for all time in order to confound the erring ones and doubters. By Saint Anthony!" he shouts. "But that fellow fucks like a master of the art."

"'Tis a most entrancing sight!" observes the Mother Abbess, watching the two with amorous eyes. "How fortunate I am to witness it," she continues.

Pampinea in the meantime had arisen, and after arranging her attire, stood with downcast eyes and flushed cheeks awaiting her sentence. The Mother Abbess however did not pay any attention to her, and acted as though she was unaware of Pampinea's presence.

"Ha! That was an excellent shove!" she shouts. "Now, Aminda, return it with interest. Hold! I will stroke his arse, and fondle his balls. Now! Now! Gardener, show your mettle!"

Pampinea was overjoyed to witness the Mother Abbess' actions. She now felt more secure as she observed the conduct of her Superior.

With his arse being slapped, his balls fondled, and his prick tightly enfolded in an hitherto unfucked cunt, Tasso was in the seventh heaven of bliss. Nature could hold back no longer.

"Come! Come!" cried Father Joachim. "Spit

the contents of thy loins into the maid. This will but half satisfy her. By Saint Anthony! I will take a hand in the game myself."

The priest was right. When Tasso removed himself Aminda endeavoured to prevent it.

"What! Through already?" she cried, regardless of the company. "Bah! I am but half satisfied! – Oh! Holy Virgin! – Give me a prick! I am burning up with desire."

Aminda was in that state of feeling that few physicians seem acquainted with. The most modest and virtuous woman, left in an unsatisfied state, would without reluctance yield herself to the embrace of her most hated foe. 'Tis now that Father Joachim finds the best field for the display of his unrivalled talents.

"Fuck her, Father! Fuck her!" cried the amorous Mother Abbess. "Tasso is dry."

The gardener was highly indignant at the thrust.

"Madame," he retorts, "were you in my place, and beseeched constantly by a dozen prick-hunters such as your nuns here, upon my soul you would not have another drop within you."

"Ha! Ha! – Nice carryings on in my convent," remarks the Mother Abbess in a serio-tragic tone. "You are the deaf and dumb man, eh? – The modest one who dared not raise your eyes in passing us, eh? – By the Blessed Mother, I will have you to fuck me and no one else, – dost hear?"

"Alas! Madame," returns Tasso. "I pray you have mercy! You know the old saying, that 'one cock will do for ten hens, but one prick will not do for a dozen women,' for be it known to you that ten stiff pricks cannot satisfy one woman. Know you also that a disorder of long standing had deprived me of hearing as well as speech. The beautiful Aminda gave me such extreme pleasure that my senses were for a time dissipated. When they returned, I found myself a perfect man again."

"We will speak further of this in the future," said the Mother Abbess. "Just now we have no further time to waste on thee. – Ha! Observe Father Joachim! – See! He has already replaced thee. How well his handsome prick fits into Aminda's little cunt! – Watch them fuck! Oh! Is it not an entrancing sight? – Ho! Father! Work thy loins! – Ha! I know you are shooting into her. Halt her screams! Stifle them, or we may have unwelcome visitors!"

Father Joachim was enjoying himself to the fullest extent. Aminda's slit was eager for a prick, and when the Father placed his splendid tool into the hot and luscious cunt, it was indeed, the extreme of happiness for both. What a glorious sight it was! And how they all enjoyed it!

81

When Father Joachim had spent copiously into Aminda, he removed his fallen prick, and dropping on his knees between her thighs, pressed unnumbered kisses upon her still excited and palpitating cunt.

"The hour is late," spoke up the Mother Abbess. "Father, it is time to cry halt. You may enjoy this more in the future. – Tasso, away to your employment. – Pampinea and Aminda, go to your apartments."

"Were it not for an important engagement elsewhere," interrupted Father Joachim, "I would give you each such a rounding up as would make you utter shrieks of joy once more."

"Well," joined in the Mother Abbess. "In a few days we will hold high revelry, and participate in such a feast as you have never heretofore dreamed of."

A loud cry of approval greeted this bit of interesting information.

"I will inform you as to it at the proper time. – Oh! By the way, I might mention that letters have been sent from Madrid informing me that the famous Monk Pedro has been appointed one of our Confessors, and is now on the way here. I expect him the coming morrow. Rumour saith that he has been sent abroad as a punishment for engaging in an illicit amour with the King's daughter. – I am anxious to test his abilities. – Now, farewell."

Speaking thus the Mother Abbess and Father Joachim slowly wended their way conventward, while Tasso departed to resume his tasks.

Pampinea and Aminda walked towards their respective apartments slowly and with a somewhat halting gait, due no doubt to a little too-much of that pleasant prick-rubbing to which they had just been subjected.

# CHAPTER VIII.

## THEY ALL TAKE A HAND IN IT

CONVENT life in Italy at the period upon which our narrative touches, was anything but one made up of sacrifice, penance and devotion. The cloak of religion was but a thin disguise for the greatest immorality, and the greater the reputation for sanctity, the deeper would the inmates plunge into lecherous pleasures. The convent was the resort of the gay and dissolute youth of the sunny clime, who indulged in orgies and dissipation that would have done no discredit to their Roman ancestors, who had long been acknowledged by those competent to decide, to be veritable adepts in arts of fucking, sucking and buggering. The ancients practically made the science of fucking a fine art, and we who follow in their footsteps are naught but mere imitators. It therefore will not cause a shock to the intelligent reader to describe at length the riotous orgies which we are about to depict, for such sensual banquets were quite common in Italy, where the hot blood courses through the veins with lightning speed, and the passions at times become so uncontrollable as to rage with the fierceness of beasts or fabled centaurs.

The Convent in which the scenes of our story lay was an exception to the rule. It possessed an enviable reputation for sanctity and was frequently quoted as an example well worthy of imitation. The larger portion of its inmates confined themselves to sacred practices only, and the fall from grace of the Mother Abbess and the younger Sisters was totally unknown.

The Mother Abbess deferred to a week later the promised feast of love.

"It will give us time to recuperate," she said to Father Joachim, who impatiently awaited the evening of joy. "That fellow Tasso has been too devoted a follower of Venus," she added, with a suggestive smile.

"Hum! Lucky dog!" said the priest, a little enviously. "He is a fine gardener! – Ha! Ha!" he laughed. "What a nice crop of brats he will leave behind him! He has planted his seed to good advantage."

"I esteem it a misfortune that I was not acquainted with his talents before," observed the Mother Abbess. "But come! I must send you on a mission. Go and bid Robina, Lucia, Pampinea and Aminda to assemble here in this room tomorrow night. – Oh! By the way, forget not our Tasso. Ambrose is already informed, – and likewise the Spanish monk, Pedro."

"Why, he has but recently come from Madrid. What know you of him?"

"He is known as the Spanish Stallion, and I am informed that none can excel him in the gentle arts of love. By our Lady! I am anxious to test his virility. I already burn and itch with desire. Oh! I must play with your prick a moment, Father."

In compliance with this request, the priest undid his cassock; and showed to the amorous woman his ponderous engine.

She seizes it with greedily lustful hands, and works it fiercely, squeezing the heavy balls. At the same time Father Joachim buries his finger in her moist crevice, and they give each other exquisite pleasure for an extended period.

Finally the Mother Abbess recovers herself.

"We must not be backwards tonight," she says, giving his prick a last gallop.

Father Joachim then departed without any further delay.

Punctually at the appointed time they all assemble in the apartment selected for the meeting. The place chosen was a room in the most unfrequented portion of the Convent. Heavy curtains hid everything from prying eyes. A banquet table, spread with delicacies and luscious fruits first met the gaze of those who entered. The Mother Abbess was seated on a throne-like chair at the head of the table, and bade a most generous welcome to every guest.

"I introduce to you, ladies and gentlemen, (for that is what I will term you this festive night,) the Monk Pedro, also called the Spanish Stallion."

Shouts of laughter greet this sally.

"I will tell you my opinion when I taste his prick," observes the virtuous Robina.

'Yes! So will we all!" chime in the other pseudo-virgins.

Soon the wine was becoming effective, for all were presently partaking freely of the generous juice of the grape.

Modestly was quickly thrown aside with the vestments. The Mother Abbess was the first to set the example. A single motion, and she was entirely disrobed. One naked leg is placed upon the table. Then she falls back, sighing.

"Come, my Spanish Stallion! Fuck me before them all."

The handsome Pedro, a tall Hercules as it were, strips himself in a trice and displays a tool worthy of his title.

"Has he not a fine prick, Robina?" says Lucia, admiringly. "I would very much like to feel it inside me!"

"I am anxious to taste of it like yourself, Lucia," returns Robina, gazing with tender looks upon the Spaniard's prick.

Meanwhile the Mother Abbess was snatching frantically at the object before her. She would squeeze it gently, then draw her hand slowly backward in a most teasing manner.

The monk was pawing at her cunt in a most ferocious way. His whole hand grasped the fat lips, and pressed them tightly. Then he would insert two fingers, and titillate her clitoris until her arse jumped convulsively.

"They are getting in fine shape for a good fuck," says Father Ambrose, taking Lucia up on his lap and inserting his stiff prick between her naked thighs. Then with his other hand, he played with Robina's cunt.

Father Joachim had placed himself in front of Pampinea's lovely font, and rapturously kissed the ruby lips.

Tasso, whose stomach was filled with good wine,

seemed to be in fine fettle. His hand strayed to that delightful slit belonging to Aminda.

"That's right! Play with my cunt, dear Tasso, while I look at Father Pedro. See!" she cries. "He is about to fuck her now. Will it not be delightful for you to play with my cunt while they are fucking?"

The Mother Abbess now lost all sense of womanly modesty, for she caught hold of the Spanish Stallion's prick and pulled him by it to a couch conveniently placed, he playing with her cunt all the while. Look! She wrestles with him, twines her limbs about him like a vine, then she falls upon the couch and raises her limbs in the air. His mighty prick enters her veteran cunt without a halt. With a fierce wrench she throws him off, pounces upon his prick with her mouth, and mumbles her prayers over it as though Priapus were her God.

"Have at her, Monk!" gleefully shouts Father Ambrose.

"Hey! Stallion, your mighty prick will be conquered this time!" cries Father Joachim.

"Yea! Yea!" chimes in Tasso. "If she does not fuck you dry, she will suck you dry!"

Monk Pedro was oblivious to such jesting. He is wild with lust. He plays with his companion's

89

splendid arse. He pushes up her ponderous titties, – squeezes, bites and sucks them.

The entranced Abbess is not a whit behind. Her tongue licks everything with which it comes into contact.

Again his prick enters her cunt. This time he will not be thrown off. He joins his stomach to hers. His big balls are close to her arse-hole. He keeps his prick in place, and moves his muscular arse from side to side.

The Mother Abbess gasps with pleasure. She cannot speak, but utters little shrieks expressive of the exquisite pleasure she is experiencing.

"See! See! He will not be halted," says Pampinea, whose arse is already quivering with delight from Father Joachim's ravishing fingering.

In vain the partly distracted Mother Abbess motions to her partner to move in and out.

"Beloved friend," observes Father Pedro, "I have her impaled, and as I am not yet ready to spend, I will stay as I am."

"By all the Saints!" shouts Ambrose. "If you will not oblige her, I will take a turn myself."

"An excellent suggestion," rejoins the Stallion.

Then he works his arse swiftly until his prick is streaming with the juices of his partner. He then withdraws his instrument, as stiff as ever.

Father Ambrose takes his place, and the Mother Abbess engulfs his prick at a single push. He rages like a bull; their bellies meet with a loud slap. Her tongue wags at him as an invitation to his own. Now they fuck with their mouths as well. His lunges are fiercely lustful, but he is not so well primed as Father Pedro. Off comes Father Ambrose with a mighty shout of unrestrained excessive bliss.

He withdraws his flabby prick and is pushed aside by the Spaniard, who again inserts his fine mettlesome steed into the willing cunt before him. He places a finger in her arse-hole and now works his backside with wonderful speed. Again she wags her tongue. He obeys the signal.

"His time is not far off!" cries Tasso.

"Nor is mine!" cries Aminda, whose clitoris is now in fine shape to be rubbed by a stiff prick.

Robina, Lucia and Pampinea are in like condition. They were all in such a state of sexual excitement that at the slightest motion, they all would have sucked their partners' pricks without a single note of protest.

"Fuck me harder!" shrieks the Mother Abbess. "Run your finger further up my arse, and work it up and down in time with your prick. Oh! Do you never mean to spend? – Hurry! I am dying

to suck your cock! Now work your finger in my arse
faster! That's it! That's something like it! – Ha! You
spend at last! – Jesu! What a stream comes from
you!"

"Ah! By Saint Iago!" shouts the now enraptured
Monk. "I am spending! I will not lose a single drop to
save your soul from perdition!"

Saying this he gave his body a violent wrench, followed by another and still more violent one.

"Once more!" he shouts, shooting his manly
offerings into the innermost recesses of her palpitating womb.

Then he glued himself to his partner, and remained
motionless for quite a period.

While the two were thus engaged, the others were
by no means idle. Father Joachim had slipped his
prick into Pampinea's tight little cunnie, and was
pushing forward and backward in the pleasantest
style imaginable.

"Your prick feels heavenly!" sighs his partner
embracing him in the most fervid manner.

"Yes, my daughter," he rejoins. "And your cunt
is so tight and warm that I wish I could fuck it a whole
day. Is it not delicious? – Now suck my lips and I will
suck yours! – That is the way! – Now gurgle your
tongue in my mouth! – I feel you spending, but that
will only make you anxious to be fucked harder."

"Oh! Father! Just look at my cunt," says Pampinea. "See! Its lips are right against your hair. If your prick was larger I could take it all in with ease."

"Yes, my daughter. It is indeed a pretty sight. Now I will not move my prick, but just put my hands across your arse and press you tightly to me. Ah! God! – But this is heavenly! I will lay you down on the couch in a few moments, and fuck you hard, – very hard. I can now feel my prick moving gently away up!"

"Oh! Father! I want a good hard fucking! But before you commence, thrust your tongue way into my mouth. There! Yes! That is the way! – Yum! Yum! Yum! – Now fuck me as hard as you are able!"

Father Joachim at once obeyed the anxious girl's request. He laid her on the couch, and gave it to her in heroic style. His fine prick would come out only to be eagerly sucked back by Pampinea's greedy cunt.

While thus engaged, the Mother Abbess had placed Pedro's fallen prick in her lecherous mouth, and was sucking it with the appetite of a hungry beast.

"A prick! A prick!" she mumbles. "A prick to fuck me!"

Gentle remonstrances come from the rest of the fair ones. For as the reader knows, there were not quite enough pricks to go round, and each one was in great demand.

Father Ambrose appeared to have his nose in Robina's cunt, while his two hands were playing with Lucia's arse and crotch as well.

"I am suffering!" shrieks the Mother Abbess. "Hasten! Oh! Hasten! I am burning up!"

Father Ambrose could not resist the appeal. He now left Robina and Lucia, and placed himself between the thighs of the Mother Abbess. Her cunt was all wet with sexual dew, but this only excited the priest onward. A lecherous cry came from him. His large and thick tool was as stiff as a rod of ivory, and in fine shape to satisfy a wanton woman. With a vigorous shove, he placed his prick home and then started to fuck with all his power.

"Ah!" cries Aminda to Tasso. "The Mother Abbess is in heaven. Look at her eyes! She appears to be enjoying herself beyond expression. She has one prick in her mouth, and another in her cunt."

"Yes!" returns Tasso, who was fucking Aminda vigorously all the while. "She ought to have something in her arse-hole, too."

"Oh! Tasso!" cries Aminda. "Turn me on my side, and then I can see the Mother Abbess being fucked whilst you fuck me."

Tasso at once complied with the request. He proceeded to give her a good prick-drubbing as she watched the others. He gave it to her so finely that Aminda's arse trembled like a leaf in the storm.

"When you get through, I must suck your prick, too," says the sobbing girl.

Tasso was also greatly excited, for as he looked about him, he saw the handsome Joachim withdraw himself from Pampinea's slit and place his prick, after bathing it in cold water, in Pampinea's mouth. She sucked it with the gusto of a child eating sweets. Robina and Lucia, left to themselves, were tickling each other's clitoris.

Tasso, with his prick in Aminda's cunt, lifted her up, and carried her to where the Mother Abbess was engaged in amorous warfare. Placing the palpitating form of his partner in close proximity to the double fucked Abbess, he ran his finger up her arse and moving it in and out of the darker fringed hole, violently fucked Aminda at the same time.

Meanwhile Pedro's prick, under the tender manipulation of the Mother Abbess' mouth, had assumed its most formidable appearance. When he withdrew his staff, it was red and swollen.

"Put it in my arse-hole," pleads the Mother Abbess, sick with lust. "Fuck my arse-hole! – Oh! For Christ's sake, fuck it!"

As she spoke, Father Ambrose uttered a hoarse shout, and emptied into her a copious supply of rich semen. He then proceeded to suck her mouth, whilst she ran her tongue down his throat.

Aminda now commenced to move her arse with quickened motions, expressive of unalloyed pleasure; for Tasso's fine prick was touching her to the very quick.

"Hurry, Tasso!" she whispered in his mouth. "I am crazy to suck your dear prick."

While she was thus speaking, Father Pedro flatly refused to obey the Mother Abbess' request.

"Two fine cunts are awaiting a prick!" he exclaimed. "I prefer cunt to arse-hole. Therefore, let Tasso's finger answer."

He spoke truly.

Robina and Lucia were reposing naked in each other's arms.

"Oh! I would give the world for a good prick," sighed Robina.

"So would I!" echoed Lucia.

The Spaniard at once went to them. Then placing their cunts on a level with his mouth, he cried,

"By Saint Peter! What glorious cunts! See this one with its jutting lips and scarlet mouth! – Ah! God! What a feast!"

He places his finger in Robina's wet cunt, and epicurean-like he rubbed and felt its satiny softness.

"Oh! What pleasure will I enjoy as I fuck this creamy thing! Sister Lucia, sit up on the couch! Open your thighs wider, and I will suck your cunt as I fuck Robina."

Placing a pillow under Robina's arse, he inserted his prick between the lips of her cunt, at the same time sucking Lucia's slit.

"Dear! Dear! Father!" cried Robina. "Your prick is thick and big! – But it feels perfectly heavenly! – See! You are nearly half-way in! – Oh! Merciful Saviour! It is all the way in! Now your big balls are against my arse!"

"You are indeed enjoying it, Robina, for you show by your countenance that your pleasure is very great. – Oh! Robina! He is sucking my cunt deliciously. Oh! Oh! – I will spend right in his mouth soon."

But Robina was speechless with the pent up bliss. The splendid prick of the Spanish Stallion was giving her the most exquisite joys on this earth. Her vagina sucked it so hard that Pedro could not stroke her quickly: – for when he drew his prick outward, the folds of her lovely cunt came with it, thus giving him indescribable pleasure. As he gazed about he also saw scenes that goaded him to the extremest point of human endurance.

Pampinea and Father Joachim had their hands between each other's thighs and a finger in their respective arse-holes. The Mother Abbess was busily engaged in sucking Father Ambrose's prick, whilst he, in turn, sucked wildly away at Aminda's hot and quivering cunt. On her part, she had Tasso's prick in her mouth, and was moulding it in the most lecherous manner. Tasso had his three fingers in the Mother Abbess' slit, and another finger in her arse-hole. Thus the entire company were now engaged in bestowing upon one another the most libidinous touches.

Lechery was rampant. Prick was king and Cunt was his consort. Here were men of great talents, and celebrated as teachers of the people. Their preachings electrified their hearers. They were looked upon as the servants of God deputed to do His will on this earth. No thoughts of an evil character were ever supposed to have strength enough to wean them for a moment from their priestly ways.

Yet look upon them! – Yea, behold them! – Where is now their boasted strength to resist temptation? Bah! Cunt conquers all men. And the saintly women, to whom a few months since the very thought of contact with man was contamination! – Now they are sucking pricks with the greatest gusto.

Lo! The pride of woman falleth before Prick. When priest and nun throw off the mask of sanctity, they display passion raging beneath with volcanic force. Fucking is but the half way post; sucking is another quarter, and buggering marks the finish.

When the Spanish Stallion had finished Robina, the nun was but partly satisfied. She commenced rolling forward and backward along the floor, gesticulating violently with both legs and arms.

Lucia was spending, and at the same time uttering deep sighs indicative of extreme desire. Her cunt had been well sucked but not yet fucked. A good stiff prick was now an absolute necessity to ease her sufferings.

Pedro saw her anxiously eyeing his prick. He understood her mute appeal. Then, after bathing his tool with fresh cool water, he placed it in her mouth. As he did so, she uttered little shrieks of delight. Finally, her suckings gave him the desired hard-on, and when he removed it from between her lips, it appeared bigger and thicker than ever.

She eyed it with the look of a famished hound, and threw her legs upward, thus exposing the blonde-haired cunnie, plump arse, and broad white thighs.

With a beastly cry the Spanish Stallion falls upon her, and plunges his prick straight into the close-mouthed red-limned mount of Venus, and works his arse without mercy. The greedy cunt takes it all in, and Lucia moves her arse from side to side, and meanwhile utters deep sighs of satisfaction.

"Spare me not, Father!" she cries. "Now fuck all you can! I feel your prick way up in me!"

"Sweet angel!" replies Pedro. "Was ever a man so blessed? Your cunt is so tight and warm that the head of my prick feels as if it were afire. Ah! Christ! Christ! – How I would like to put my balls into you! – Come here, Robina! Let me suck your cunt while I fuck Lucia."

Robina places herself in a position to gratify the lecherous priest, and soon he is sucking away for dear life. His big prick at the same time, is rushing in and out of Lucia's greedy cunt, with speedy thrusts.

The whole apartment now resounded with shouts of vulgar language.

"A prick for my arse-hole!" still pleads the Mother Abbess.

Alas for her! No sodomite is there to gratify her. There are too many enticing cunts in opposition.

Such scenes as we now depict may seem as unreal as they are unnatural; but the keen student of human nature knows well that the most modest of women, when over-excited by a good fucking, will halt at nothing. In their cooler moments, they would be horrified at the very thought, rather than act in the manner in which the present pages now suggest.

# CHAPTER IX.

## A PRINCESS HAD TO HAVE IT

FOR A short period the company halted. Over-excited nature now demanded a brief respite. Through the forethought of the Mother Abbess, utensils for ablution were plentiful. Priests and nuns could be seen gently bathing pricks and cunts in order to strengthen them for renewed orgies. Wines and light refreshments abounded. Naked forms sat around the banquet board. Shafts of wit with pointed allusions brought forth paroxysms of laughter.

'The arse-hole is still waiting!" shouts Ambrose. "Who will be the first to storm the breach?"

"Yes! Yes!" returns the Mother Abbess. (The wine-glass had been raised perhaps too often to her lips.) "I will take a prick in my mouth, another in my cunt, and still another in my arse-hole!"

"Be not so greedy!" cry the others, indignantly. "Would you deprive us all to gratify yourself?"

"Have no fear, fair Sisters," interjects Joachim. "It would take a regiment to gratify our Mistress. She is a veritable succubus. 'More! More!' is her ever constant cry."

A shout of laughter greets this sally.

"Cunts were formed for fucking, and pricks were made to fuck them!" chimes in Father Pedro. "If it were not so, God would have given us little holes to piss out of. But arse-holes were made for still another purpose, and I for one, have no desire to put my tool in such a dirty place!"

"Bravo! Bravo!" shout the anti-sodomites approvingly.

The Mother Abbess laughed loud and mockingly, in a perfect fit of mirth.

Father Joachim endeavoured to restrain the outburst.

"Madame, I beseech you not to give way to your feelings in such loud tones. We may awake the aged Sisters."

"Quiet your fear," returned the Mother Abbess, restraining her mirth somewhat. "Think you that I have not prepared against such an event? We are now in the unused portion of the Convent.

103

The other Sisters are locked securely in their cells."

[Father Joachim, Pedro and Ambrose, be it known to you, were not residents of the Convent. They were supposed to dwell in a monastery some distance removed from their present location. Their vocation as Confessors' however, gave them special privileges, and as the reader will observe, they were by no means backward in taking advantage of the opportunities offered them.]

The entire company now became lost to all sense of shame. Once more modesty was thrown to the winds. For wine and full stomachs have a tendency to influence the passions; and the present instance was no exception to the rule.

Would that a painter's skilled hand could depict in glowing colours what the pen is now incapable of fully describing. The beautiful maidens were now mere animals. Plump white thighs were partly lolling on the table and chairs, the atmosphere being so balmy that nakedness was pleasant. Pouting cunts were displaying themselves in such a manner as would have influenced even a hermit, or corrupted a saint, – and the Fathers present were neither. Their hands were playing with the tempting lips and clitoris of each. Deep sighs indicative of exquisite pleasure came from all. Pricks and balls were being handled in the most lascivious manner. Lily-white arses were gently rising up and down in the anticipation of the joys that were to come.

"Ah!" said Father Pedro, whose sturdy tool and large rounded appendages were worked at once by Robina and Lucia. "This is almost as fine as my palace experiences."

This remark attracted the attention of all.

"You excite our curiosity," chimes in the Mother Abbess. "Come, tell us the story. From whence comes your title of Stallion?"

"Yes! Yes!" cry the rest in unison. "Tell us the story."

Father Pedro smiled.

"I will relate to you the cause of the title," he replied. "But soft! Before I commence, sweet Sisters," he added, turning to Lucia and Robina, "restrain your eagerness. Handle me gently, and I will entertain each of your cunts in return. This pleasant dalliance must last until I finish my tale."

Then the entire company, whilst dallying with one another, listened to the following narrative:

"I scarcely need remind you," commenced the narrator, "that for ages the Spaniards have been renowned as adepts in the arts of love as well as of war. Hot blooded and impulsive, addicted to strong jealousies, it is said of us that we are more prone to punish than to reward. A Spaniard will imperil his life and honour for a woman's embrace, yet he will pursue with implacable vengeance the outrager of his domestic hearth. He receives but will make no return. Secrecy is safety – discovery is ruin.''

"Bah!" interrupted Father Ambrose. "Have done with such dry details. Come to the point without so much wandering.''

Pedro flushed deeply at the reproof, if such it might be termed. But an extra jerk of his prick by Robina restrained his temper.

"Know then, that in Madrid I was in the employ of his Eminence the Cardinal, as Secretary. My employment brought me frequently to the Palace, and it was not long before I was on excellent terms with the King and the entire royal family.

"My conduct was of the most exemplary character; and I was looked upon as a model of propriety. Such was the confidence displayed in me that I became a depository for all the secrets of the Palace. I acted the part of Confessor to the best of my ability, and reproved and rewarded in turn.

"One afternoon I was summoned to the Cardinal's private apartments, and to my great astonishment, was addressed as follows:

"'Father Pedro, you know that we who serve the Holy Father obey him in all things, halting not to inquire the why and wherefore. Therefore, my son, be not amazed at what I now speak of to you. Learn that the Princess Dolores, the fairest maid in all Spain, is in a delicate situation. Her physician informs me that she must perforce have sexual connection without delay, or her life may pay the forfeit. – Do you follow me?'"

"'Perfectly, your Eminence,' I replied.

"'Well,' continued the Cardinal, 'a month hence she will be married to the Prince of Parma. But pending that period, her condition is so serious that nothing but a man can alleviate it. Now the marriage of the Prince and the Princess is of absolute importance, for the reason that the Church will vastly benefit by it. Should the death of the Princess prevent such a consummation, the Holy Father will be overwhelmed with grief. He has set his heart upon this union, as vast interests can thus be maintained. – But, enough of explanations. I now order you to go to the Princess this very evening, and give her that relief which nature so strenuously demands. We know we are safe when we confide in thee. We dare not seek another. What sayest thou, my son?'

" 'To hear is to obey,' I responded humbly, with head bowed and raised hands clasped in prayer.

"With a gesture, the Cardinal dismissed me.

"Now laugh as you will, Brothers and Sisters. Nevertheless, I speak truth when I state that heretofore I had never enjoyed a woman, save in imagination. You well know," he added, with a suggestive smile, "that our text-books which we striplings studied before our entrance into the priesthood, are crowded with descriptive and alluring suggestions. A hundred or more volumes are devoted solely to subjects of a sexual nature, and I can assure you that they can with truth be termed 'An Exposition of the Art of Fucking' in every shape, manner, and form known to civilized and uncivilized nations.

"The maiden I was about to satisfy was the most beautiful woman in Spain. The young gallants of Madrid would have periled their lives and fortunes to obtain her. Yet here was I offered this luscious fruit without an effort."

"Lucky dog!" quoth Ambrose, between his set teeth. "How I envy you!"

A murmur of disapproval quieted the interloper.

It was evident that the company were becoming greatly interested.

"I prepared myself fittingly for the coming event," resumed Father Pedro. "The perfumed bath of the King was at my disposal that evening; for upon my arrival at the Palace, a lovely maid of honour met me and conducted me to that apartment.

"'I have been commanded by high authority,' quoth she, with a smile upon her lovely face, 'not to lose sight of thee until the destination is reached.'

"And you may be assured she obeyed her commands faithfully. She saw me disport naked in the bath. With gloating looks did she observe my manly beauties, and it was only with great difficulty that she could restrain herself from fondling me.

"When I entered the private chamber of the Princess, I saw the beautiful being reposing on a couch of great magnificence. Two maids of honour were in attendance upon her.

"Previous to my entrance I had not allowed my thoughts to dwell on the subject. I saw only the path of duty. Passion had not yet commenced to play its part.

"The Princess was attired in a silken robe; but

when I fell upon my knees I saw that it covered nakedness only. For when she gave me her hand to kiss, the robe revealed the superb bosom entirely to my gaze. By all the saints!" cried the enraptured Pedro. "Never did I see such a beautiful being! Her white skin would have matched the purest alabaster. Her long black hair fell to her feet. Her coal black eyes pierced me like an arrow's dart. Her cheeks were suffused with the deepest crimson, and her reddened lips were a Cupid's bow, wet with dew.

"I fell upon those lips like a famished dog. I sucked and sucked the velvet mouth, and was sucked in return, for the Princess was overflowing with desire.

"'Pardon my sin, Father,' she whispered softly.

"'The Virgin herself would atone for thee! – Oh! Lovely Princess,' I returned.

"Regardless of the arch-looks of the maids of honour present, I threw off my single garment. The Princess in turn imitates me, and there, naked and palpitating, does she lie before me. With eager hands I seize upon the hemispheres before me, and mumbling cries of excited lust as I press and fondle them, and suck their virgin rubies, and press unnumbered kisses alternately on lips and bosom;

while she, with both hands upon my gloriously stiffened prick, is uttering cries indicative of unbridled lasciviousness.

"Our lips join in one long, long kiss. Our tongues stick together. Then I halt to gaze upon the beauties lower down. – Ah! God! – Sisters!" he cries, halting in his narrative, "Have mercy! Permit me to finish this story with stiffened tool."

"I cannot help myself, Father," returns Lucia.

"Nor yet can I," adds Robina. "Your fingering excites me so greatly that I lose command of myself."

"You break in upon his narrative," cries the Mother Abbess. "Contain yourselves, Sisters. Let us have no more interruption."

"Where was I?" asks Pedro, bewildered.

"You were just about to gaze upon the beauties lower down!" cry Ambrose, Joachim and Tasso in one voice.

A shout of laughter greets this involuntarily concerted answer.

"Ah! Yes!" resumed Pedro. "I gazed at the sight before me like a famished wolf. The white stomach, the magnificent thighs which were opening and shutting in gleeful anticipation, but best of all the mount of Venus, the door of Paradise, the sweet silken-lined cunt. Between its moist and reddened lips nestled a half-blown rose, a symbol of virginity that Princesses of Spain have worn from the beginning of their history. None but a true virgin dare place a bud in such a receptacle.

"I uttered a shriek of delight at this most enchanting sight, removed the bud, and alternately kissed and sucked the unfucked slit. Then I played with the exquisite clitoris until the couch groaned with her motions and tossings.

"My prick was now swollen to an enormous extent. As I glanced at it, I heard a voice say:

"'The King's Stallion cannot compare with it.'

"It was the maid on the left who spoke. It was then that I became aware that the two whom I first saw upon my entrance, were still in attendance.

"'Ah! My mistress will be split apart by such a monster!'

"'Have no fear!' retorts the other. 'She will conquer it shortly, and reduce it to nothingness.'

"The Princess meanwhile was mad with passion. She pulls me vigorously towards her. I mount her, like the stallion that I am. My staff is burning with desire. I push open the tightly closed lips of the royal slit. Not a protest comes from her.

Now I am in. I rage like a bull. I push. I snort. She bids me onward. I fuck and fuck. She foams at the mouth. I fuck and fuck more swiftly than before. My feet are on the floor. I am in a glorious position between her thighs. She then raises her feet, and places them upon my shoulders. Still I fuck and fuck until my balls are all but in the breach. Then I pause for breath.

"A loud shriek, expressive of overflowing joys, comes from her. Then I pounce upon her mouth and suck the sweetness from her lips.

"Thus glued together, I unloosed the long pent-up savings of my loins, and pour them into her inmost depths, so much so as to copiously drench every portion of her womb. Yet I did not withdraw myself. She seeks to throw me off. In vain! I fuck and fuck, she wildly gesticulating with her arms, and pressing me close with her dainty feet.

"Thus we lay, – how long I know not, nor cared. If I could have stayed thus, never would I have removed myself; but as such things must have an end, so it came in my case, too.

"'Ha!' cries one of the maids. 'Did I not speak truth? See! She has conquered it completely.'

"The Princess was lying in sweet confusion upon the couch. Her attendants did her needed service, and later, I too, was treated like a royal prince. Ere that night of pleasure had ended, I had fucked both the virgin maids of honour, each in turn, straight before the royal face.

"'As these faithful maids have honoured me, so I will honour them!' cries the Princess. 'Father!' she added, 'See! They await your pleasure!'

"By the ten thousand virgins!" swore Pedro. "How I did fuck them! And their sobs of joy linger in my ears even yet! And for a finale, the Princess with her dainty mouth sucked my hard-worked prick into an erect state, and in return I gave her such a bouncing as to completely drive all sickness entirely from her.

"Need I say more? Save that the Prince of Parma espoused the Princess of Spain a month later, and my master complimented me highly for the assistance I had lent in the affair. Some of the details in a mysterious manner became known in Church channels. Hence the title given me."

That Father Pedro's story was highly appreciated needs scarce to be mentioned. All present were infatuated with the tale. The orgies recommenced with renewed vigour, and the apartment witnessed

114

scenes in which unbridled lust figured to an extent unimaginable even to the most depraved of human beings.

Aminda could be seen handling Tasso's fine prick with such vigorous jerks that it seemed as if she would dissever it from his body. He in turn was sucking her burning slit. He imprints long and hot kisses upon it. He implores her to have mercy upon his instrument of pleasure.

"Give me your cunt to fuck!" he begs.

She answers by throwing herself upon his tool, and fucks him with such gusto that he writhes about like a serpent.

Father Pedro has secured a stout birch, and commences to give the Mother Abbess' large fat arse a sound drubbing.

Lucia, Robina and Pampinea are chasing the naked priests Joachim and Ambrose around the apartment. Soon the five forms are intermingled. Cunts and pricks are fondled with eager touches. The prick of Ambrose enters Lucia's cunt. Joachim fucks Pampinea, while Robina enjoys the pleasure of having her cunt sucked in turn by the two priests.

Pedro is once more in superb shape. His large prick inflames the Mother Abbess to passions beyond control. She sucks it until it dwindles to flabbiness, and so the company enjoyed themselves until the faint beams of the rising sun bade them to disperse.

# CHAPTER X.

## ROSA WINDS IT UP

THE lascivious pleasures which were so greatly enjoyed by all who were present at the amorous orgies just described in our last chapter, were unfortunately never repeated; for, a few days later Fathers Joachim, Pedro and Ambrose received summons from those high in authority, commanding their presence elsewhere.

The Mother Abbess and the Sisters were deeply grieved when the Fathers informed them of this fact.

"Alas!" cried the Mother Abbess, as she affectionately embraced in turn each of these departing priests. "Who shall now give our hungry cunts solace? It was only this very morning that our Tasso left for a month's absence. His aged parent is in a decline, and needs his son's presence to cheer his dying hours."

"Ah!" sighed the beautiful Robina. "What ill fortune is ours!"

"Restrain your grief," said Father Pedro, mournfully, "or you will but add to our own."

The three Fathers then and there fucked the Mother Abbess and the four Sisters until the entire party were deluged with blissful feelings. They fucked and sucked until exhaustion forced them all to halt.

After the departure of the lusty monks, affairs in the Convent resumed their usual state. Two attenuated, wrinkled Friars now acted the part of Confessors. They were lean and shrivelled, and in strong contrast to the strong and sturdy monks whom they had succeeded.

The Mother Abbess was loud in her complaints.

"How dare they inflict such scarecrows upon us?" she protested, indignantly, to the Sisters.

"Their stinking breaths show that their stomachs are starved with improper food," interjected Lucia.

"And one of them," spoke up Aminda, "bade me to sacrifice my appetite and not indulge it so freely."

"The dastards!" exclaimed the Mother Abbess. "They would have our stomachs as foul as their own. I am of the opinion that their shrunken tools would not secure an erection, even if we were to attempt the disgusting task of trying."

"Horrid thought!" said Lucia, laughing. "No doubt," she added, "but they are so virtuous that they fail to pay attention to the calls of nature."

"Then say I," rejoins the Mother Abbess, "may they foul themselves to perdition with their own urine."

Sad indeed were the straits in which the unfortunate band of Sisters now found themselves.

"'Tis more than we can bear," said Aminda to the Mother Abbess some time afterwards. "Pampinea and myself are determined to leave this life. We shall go out into the world, find proper husbands, and be fucked every night."

"Oh! Will not that be truly delightful?" returned the Mother Abbess.

Shortly afterwards they carried out their determination and both were fortunate enough to secure lusty gallants as husbands, who, no doubt to their great satisfaction, plowed them well.

The Mother Abbess, with Lucia and Robina were now forced to seek gratification in each other's company. They often fucked one another in the feminine manner, with tongue and finger, and thus to some extent made up for the loss of the Fathers and Tasso.

About this time, an addition was made to their company in the shape of a beautiful young girl, Rosa by name. She had sought the Convent to escape the machinations of those related to her. A deceased uncle had left her a snug fortune, the possession of which had excited the envy of those closely allied to her. To free herself from their persecutions, she had fled to the Convent.

Lucia and Robina were soon on intimate terms with her.

"She is truly a virgin," said Lucia to her companion. "It was but yesterday that I asked her if she knew what prick meant. – She immediately answered in the negative.

"'Prick is what men possess,' I explained, 'It is soft at first, but when a woman touches it, the thing grows large and stiff.'

"'Oh! Yes!' she responded. 'I know now. You mean that which a man pees with. I did not quite understand at first.'

"I asked her if she knew what a cunt was, and she replied in the negative as before. When I told her, she blushed scarlet. I then spoke of the great pleasure to be obtained by joining prick with cunt, and then I further said,

"'If you will let me, I will play with your cunt to give you some conception of what would happen

120

when a man lies in bed with you.' And Oh!" continued Lucia, hotly, "would you believe it? She permitted me to play with her cunt for a long time. It made me sick with pleasure, and I told her to play with my slit as I did with hers; and soon our arses were bounding away in a manner that would set a man crazy to behold."

"I must play with her too," interrupted Robina, in an eager tone.

"Oh! She is so fresh and sweet!" returned Lucia, "that I would love to see her fucked for the first time!"

"Happy thought!" cried Robina. "You know Tasso returns tomorrow. Would it not be an excellent idea to have him fuck her? A month's absence must have given him renewed strength."

"I will make mention of it to him," replied Lucia.

The next day when Tasso returned, Lucia brought Sister Rosa to him as he was working in the garden with the old gardener. Tasso saw the signal and went at once to her.

The novice was much pleased with the appearance of the gardener; and when Robina and Lucia had told her what he had done to them, she too seemed desirous of testing his ability to please.

"We are all nearly starved," said Robina to

Rosa. "Our cunts are just watering for a man; but we will restrain ourselves in order that you may enjoy the bliss of being fucked. It will also be a source of great pleasure to the Mother Abbess if you will permit her to see you fucked by Tasso."

Now Rosa was as tempting a piece of woman-flesh as the eye of mortal man ever beheld. She was short and plump in figure, with a lovely face, expressive of a mirthful disposition. Her blue eyes were large and lustrous; and there was that in them which would make any healthy man's prick rise very quickly. The lily and the rose fought for supremacy in her cheeks, and the luscious red mouth was one to gloat over, to sigh for, to dream about.

Tasso fell head over heels in love with Rosa at first sight, and when Lucia told him of the feast she had in store for him, he knelt at her feet in worship. He raised her robe and kissed her tempting slit, whilst she in turn played with his fine prick.

"We have determined to deny ourselves," she said, removing herself from him. "You must save yourself for Rosa."

The following evening the Mother Abbess, in company with Lucia, Robina and Rosa, assembled in the apartment which had been the scene of their former orgies. Tasso did not keep them waiting;

for hardly had the four entered than he made his appearance.

The blushing Rosa was as first quite backward, but the hot-blooded Tasso soon cured her bashfulness; for he pressed her tempting bosom and played with her tight little cunt until she was in a high state of sexual excitement.

The Mother Abbess and the two Sisters will now describe the exciting contest.

"See! Tasso is quite naked!" says Robina. "How large his prick looks! – Oh! Rosa! How your backside will jump up and down when his thing is in you!"

"Rosa is bashful! She still has her gown on. – There! That is right, Tasso! Take it off and fuck her naked!"

"Look at her swelling slit! – Is it not lovely?" observes the Mother Abbess. "Tasso likes it! – See him kiss it! – That's right, Rosa. Move your arse about! – There! Lay down upon the couch! Tasso will now work your clitoris until you spend."

"Oh! This is a feast!" interjects Tasso, as he sucks Rosa's mouth, and rubs her cunt in a vigorous manner.

"Play with his balls, Rosa! – Yes! In that manner! For it will make his prick stiffer," advises Robina.

"They are both getting in shape for a good fuck!" she continues. "Look, Mother! Rosa has commenced to spend."

"Play with my cunt, both of you!" entreats the Mother Abbess, who was now in a high state of excitement.

"Tasso, do not tease her so! Her cunt is eager for your prick!" expostulated Lucia. "That is proper," she continues. "See, Robina! His prick is going in, and Rosa is pushing her arse forward! – She wants it so badly."

"How closely her cunt clings to his prick!" said Robina, who was watching the two with eager eyes.

"Oh! God! – This is pleasure, indeed!" shouts Tasso. "Her cunt is like a vice! – Oh! Ah! Ah! My balls will burst with bliss!"

"Now fuck her, Tasso! Fuck her!" almost shrieks the Mother Abbess. "Your big prick has opened her fresh cunt for the first time! – That is why it is so tight."

"His prick is all wet!" says Robina. "She must be spending."

"Ah! My finger is all wet also," cries Lucia. "Mother, you too have come off!"

"Oh! Do but see him!" admiringly exclaims the Mother Abbess. "Ah! That thrust touched her to the very quick!"

And indeed, so it seemed, for the beautiful Rosa became wild with bliss; and when Tasso halted a moment, she twisted herself on top of him and fucked and fucked him until she had drained him entirely.

When he removed his prick the three waiting women took possession of it; and when they were through, poor Tasso was as weak as a cat.


The day following, Rosa, in company with Tasso, fled from the Convent. Tasso feared that he would fade away into a veritable shadow if he continued to dwell amongst such amorous women.

Tasso and Rosa were married without delay, and continued faithful to one another for the remainder of their lives. A large family of children blessed them.

A few weeks after the flight of Tasso, Robina and Lucia followed his example, and were espoused later by two noble gentlemen, who frequently wondered at their wives' marvellous knowledge of the art of fucking. Of course the modest girls always kept them in a complete state of ignorance respecting the school in which they were so ably taught.

The Mother Abbess one day horrified her Confessor with a vulgar remark. The poor woman had been deprived of sexual food so long that she was scarcely conscious of her words.

She saluted him with the following:

"Scarecrow! Your stinking breath would shame a shit-house!"

The horrified priest at once reported this remark to his Superiors, but before the resultant penalty had time to be announced to the Mother Abbess, she had gathered up her belongings, and returned, like a sensible woman, to the world. As she was possessed of large means, and thus being able to gratify her desires, she hired ponderous footmen; and when they were fucked out, she would present them with a handsome stipend, and replace them with others more sturdy. She maintained this state for long years, occasionally varying her diet with a good fat oily friar, until finally her dwelling-place became known to the curious as a "place where fat men got thin," or, in modern parlance, an anti-fat cure. But, as death comes to all, so in due time he came to the Mother Abbess. Her place of burial is celebrated to this day in consequence of the curious monument that ornaments her last resting place. It is an immense stone, partly rounded, and a very close imitation of a stiff prick. Thus can be seen, even the ruling passion strong in death.

126

# EXTRACT FROM THE MINUTES

At a stated meeting of the *Société des Beaux Esprits* held on the 15th November 1897, the following report was submitted.

Your committee on Antiquarian Research, in submitting its report desires to call the attention of the members of the Society once more to the bequest of the late M. Jerome, a former member.

M. Jerome made a most generous bequest to us in 1896 of a large sum of money to be expended, as his will read "in the investigation of doubtful claims of authors who presume to wear borrowed plumes and thus filch the brain-work of honest though less known writers, with particular reference to authors and works named in a memorandum placed in the hands of the Secretary of the aforesaid Society."

Your committee desires to state that in pursuance of these duties, it has made a careful search not only through the libraries of the Louvre in Paris, but also the public and private libraries of London, Berlin, Florence, Rome, Milan, and divers other places, as well as our beloved city Bruxelles; and after with due care weighing the arguments for and against, we have arrived at the conclusion that the celebrated tale, Novel 1, of the third day of the *Decameron*, (familiarly known as "Masetto and the Nuns,") written by a certain Giovanni Boccaccio, and likewise several weaker imitations, owe their origin to the present work which we now lay before you, entitled *Lascivious Scenes in the Convent*. Our subcommittee has carefully and freely translated this work from the original Tuscan, into English and French, modernising it to such an extent that persons even of mean capacity may read it understandingly.

All of which is respectfully submitted.

THE COMMITTEE.

The report having been adopted, it was unanimously decided to place it upon the minutes of the Society, and the Committee was thereupon discharged from further action.

# Part II

# The Memoirs of Suzon (1778)

SUZON, THE PRETTY YOUNG HEROINE OF THESE
MEMOIRS, HAS BEEN SEDUCED AND MADE PREG-
NANT BY AN UNSCRUPULOUS ABBÉ, HER GOD-
MOTHER'S SPIRITUAL ADVISER. HE IS BRINGING THE
YOUNG WOMAN TO PARIS IN ORDER TO AVOID A
SCANDAL.

The movement of the carriage had so much advanced
my pregnancy that I was obliged to stop at some
leagues from Paris because I had entered into labour.
Abbé Fillot chose this moment to acquaint me that it
was not so much consideration for my reputation as
fear of exciting Madame d'Inville's jealousy which had
prompted him to help me. For I had barely installed
myself in a nearby inn when that infamous scoundrel
took himself off and I have never set eyes on him since.

A lady who dwelt in the neighbourhood was moved
to compassion by my piteous state and she had me
conveyed to the Hôtel Dieu[1] at Paris. Hardly had I
recovered from the rigours of giving birth, than I was
ordered to depart, taking my few wretched belongings
with me. As my reader will no doubt realise, without

1. The oldest hospital in Paris, standing beside the church of
Notre-Dame.

money my state was truly wretched. Or, to express myself in another fashion, I did not know which way to turn.

Although my state of health was still much enfeebled, I passed the day wandering around almost all the quarters of Paris without any notion where I was going. At last, worn out with fatigue and hunger, I stopped in front of a wine-merchant's shop. Reflecting then upon my misfortunes, my tears flowed abundantly. The wine-merchant's young assistant, who at that moment was standing in the entrance, taking the air, approached me and with the greatest courtesy addressed me thus:

'Mademoiselle, may I, without being indiscreet, ask the cause of your tears?'

'Ah, Monsieur!' cried I, 'it seems to me that there is not a girl in the whole world to be pitied more than myself! I was brought here by a monster who has abandoned me! I have just been turned out of the Hôtel Dieu, I have not a penny to my name and, as a crowning misfortune, have not a single acquaintance in this town.'

My frank manner, my youth and whatever beauty I possessed engaged his interest in my favour. He invited me to enter the shop and immediately served me with a generous glass of his best wine. He fetched me a bowl of steaming soup from a nearby eating establishment and pressed me so earnestly to eat that at last I yielded. After I had taken some nourishment:

'I cannot lodge you here,' said he. 'This place is only what in Paris we call a town cellar, of which I have the charge. But I shall give you the name of an inn and pay whatever it may cost.'

When I had finished the soup and drunk a few glasses of wine, perceiving that I was fatigued, he acquainted me with the whereabouts of an inn and gave me a letter for mine host in which he said I was a relative. He spoke so warmly in my favour that the people at the inn treated me with every possible consideration.

Not a day went by without my visiting my benefactor. Every day he gave me some new mark of kindness. I found so much honesty in his behaviour, that I soon fell in love with him.

For several days he had been begging me to respond to his love, which he described in such sincere terms that I was only waiting for him to become a little more pressing in order to satisfy him. At last the happy moment arrived.

One evening, just as I was about to take my leave, he invited me to descend to the cellar with him. I suspected that his purpose in so doing was not simply to show me how tidy he kept it. As our hearts were in accord, I needed no pressing and went of my own free will, although there was no doubt in my mind as to his intentions. From the way he started to caress me as soon as we arrived there, it was easy to see what he wanted, but I pretended not to know. The place was not really suitable for what the young man had in mind, but necessity was the mother of invention.

He began by handling my bosom and devouring it with kisses. Another hand slipped under my skirt and began to explore other attractions, yet all that was but a sort of prelude to what he really wanted to do. I made some difficulty, just for the sake of appearances, for my desire was at least as keen as his. I complained about the liberties he was taking but all that I could do to defend myself served only to increase his ardour. Finally, noticing that we were near a barrel, he took me in his arms and placed me on top of it. Then, situating himself between my thighs, he pulled up my petticoats. Immediately the young man brought out of his breeches a prick fit to give pleasure to the least amorous of women and plunged it up to the hilt into my cunt. Although that part of my body was still sensible after my recent ordeal, it was not long before I began to feel the approach of pleasure. My dear Nicholas (that was the lad's name) was pushing so hard that had not my back been supported by the wall, I should have been quite unable to sustain his thrusts. He was holding my legs under his arms so that, pulling me to him at the same time he was thrusting forward with his bum, there was in truth not an inch of his prick which did not enter my cunt.

After three ample discharges without uncunting, and all the time in the same posture, we ceased our pretty game, well satisfied the one with the other, and promised each other that we should recommence our exertions the next day.

This agreeable mode of life might have continued much longer if the wine-merchant, who some ill-natured person had informed of our activities, had not threatened Nicholas with dismissal if he did not immediately put an end to our liaison. This honest lad, whose love for me was as great as mine for him, was quite unable to acquaint me with this devastating news without shedding many bitter tears. His chagrin was so great and appeared so sincere that, though I myself was inconsolable, I felt obliged to try to console him.

'What is to become of you,' said he, 'if we are forced to part?'

'I will return to my family,' said I, 'and let me assure you, my beloved, that the remembrance of your kindness shall ever be dear to me.'

Since my lover knew that this must be our last meeting, he had brought with him all the money which he possessed and, with the generosity which was so characteristic of him, offered it to me. I was unwilling to accept all of the sum and could be persuaded to take only four louis, which seemed a sufficient amount to see me on my way. That very day I reserved a place in the coach and set out upon my journey two days later.

The persons who were in the public conveyance were of very varied conditions. There were monks, abbés, officers and I was the only woman. During the journey, various subjects were discussed – very superficially, as is the way on such occasions. The officers spoke about their campaigns, the abbés about their good fortune in affairs of the heart. The monks, however, during this time, did not waste words and occupied themselves with paying court to me.

Among them there was a friar who was particularly pressing. During dinner, he made me a very advantageous proposition. He said that he would give me the money to rent a little house in a village close to the monastery where he would be living, that he would support me so well that I should be obliged in all fairness to praise his generosity, and that he could make my fortune. A perfectly natural desire to be my own mistress, and the fear of being discovered and sent back to my godmother's house after an absence which must have caused a great scandal, made this proposition seem extremely attractive to me.

Having concluded that he would give me an allowance of one hundred louis, not counting the little extra presents he had promised, we agreed that a preliminary payment should be made upon the occasion of our first lying together.

We had a care to choose two bedchambers which were contiguous in the hostelry where we were staying. It was nigh on one o'clock of the morning when I heard the friar give the signal which we had agreed upon. I opened the door with the least possible noise and he entered immediately. He had brought an excellent bottle of champagne with him, of which we soon disposed. Even as the lecherous monk was drinking, he was at the same time removing the fichu which covered my bosom and unlacing me. He went into ecstasies at the sight of my breasts, which in truth were very round, very firm and white as alabaster. Then, observing that I still seemed too much attired, he served me as my maid. Evidently, he was a true monk, and this was by no means the first time he had done such things. The libidinous man would not even let me retain my chemise, saying that it was his wish to see all my charms clearly.

As soon as I was completely naked, he made me lie down on the bed, on my back first, then face downwards. Then, holding a flickering candle in his hand, he examined all parts of my body, lingering over some of them in a manner which was very agreeable for him and applying passionate kisses everywhere.

At last, after having feasted his eyes and his hands, my lover and I sealed our bargain on the bed, several times, to our entire satisfaction.

As it was necessary for us to rise early the next morning, the monk withdrew to his own bedchamber. As for me, it was not long before slumber overtook me. The next day we left the coach after a distance of about two leagues, being obliged to quit the main road to reach the village where I should henceforth be dwelling. Our travelling companions, to whom I had acquainted our destination, were much surprised to see me descend with the monk. They appeared to be quite astonished at seeing me take the same road as him. An officer, being unable to contain his vexation, called out:

'You did not acquaint us that it was your intention to enrol the young lady in your order, father. If you were not a monk, I should demand satisfaction for the insult you have offered to myself and these other gentlemen.'

The monk showed more interest in putting distance between himself and the officer than in replying to the latter's gibes. The other monks said nothing but appeared furious to see the prey they had singled out for themselves filched from under their noses. As for me, I took my leave of the company by making them a deep curtsy.

As we made our way towards the village, my monk told me that he was conducting me to the house of one of his lady penitents, and that he would ask her to lodge me until such time as a suitable house could be found for my accommodation. He said that it would be prudent on my part to make a great display of virtue to that lady in order to hoodwink her.

When we arrived, the friar told her that he had frequently seen me at the house of some mutual friends in Paris, where he had learned that, since losing my husband, I desired to live in the country in order to improve my health. That he had advised me to choose the neighbourhood of his monastery for preference, as much for the excellence of the air as for the countryside, which was, it is true, charming, and that he had at last prevailed upon me to select that place. The lady received me with great courtesy, and I remained with her for eight days, which were employed in preparing the house which I was to occupy.

During that time, not a day passed without my friar coming to visit me. As his visits to that lady had been almost as frequent before my arrival, her suspicions were never aroused. And, besides, we both behaved with a great deal of prudence and caution.

As I was not deficient in at least some knowledge of religion, I always contrived to converse on that subject whenever I was with the good lady. Thus, without making a great display of piety, I soon led her to think of me as a very virtuous woman. What pleased her, she told the friar one day, was to see that my piety in no way diminished the gaiety of my disposition. So well did I play the part of Tartuffe, that my lover's penitent never spoke of me except to sing my praises.

As soon as all was ready in my little house, I went to take possession of it, accompanied by my new friend, who stayed to dine with me, as well as my monk. He never took a meal in my house but that Madame Marcelle (that was the lady's name) was also of the party. She herself expressed her admiration of the manner with which I managed to accord my pleasures with my reputation. The friar ceaselessly assured me of

172

his amazement that one as young as I should be capable of so much prudence. Madame Marcelle was then the dupe of her Confessor's false piety and my hypocrisy. In a manner of speaking, she played the bawd for us, without the least realisation of what she was doing.

For six years I lived in that village esteemed by all the respectable people there. Never was a dinner given to which I was not invited; everyone vied with his neighbour to have the honour of my acquaintance. Husbands held me up to their wives as an example of virtue, and the mothers did the same with their daughters.

Undoubtedly, the reader is extremely curious to know how the friar and I managed to see each other in private without our liaison being discovered. He has no doubt that everything I was doing was only to give a varnish of decency to the most disorderly conduct. But did not gratitude also oblige me to safeguard my lover's reputation? Besides, should I have kept him long had I behaved differently?

In order to avoid boring those who may read these memoirs, I shall no longer postpone the satisfaction of their curiosity. This was the way of it.

Father Hercules (that was the friar's name) was the senior monk in the monastery. You may guess that, this being so, he enjoyed a much greater degree of freedom than the other monks. As he himself had chosen the house where I was living, he had given the preference to one which possessed a garden backing on to the open countryside. A gate at the end of the garden to which, naturally, he had a key, facilitated his nocturnal visits. When the monks had retired to their cells, Father Hercules left the monastery, entered by the garden gate and came to join me in my bed. Thus we spent every night together, if one overlooks a few which he judged necessary to the re-establishment of his vigour. The next morning, he would take his leave at a very early hour and return to the monastery without anyone having perceived his absence. How many delightful nights we passed together in this manner!

So much did I vary our pleasures, in so many ways did I provoke him to respond to my ardent desires, that at last I reduced the hapless monk to impotence. At length, exasperated at always finding between his legs a prick which was as slack and soft as a piece of wet rag, and disheartened by continually playing with it to no purpose, I resolved to give him an aide-de-camp. Thus I was myself the cause of all the misfortunes which have since befallen me and I have paid dearly for my ingratitude and the imprudence of my new lover.

It was not long before my choice was made. Whenever I attended mass in the monastery chapel, it had not escaped my notice that the organist always regarded me in a manner which plainly revealed the desire which he felt for me. He was a strapping fellow of a most healthy appearance who seemed eminently suitable to content a woman who had such a propensity for fucking as myself. The only problem was how to find a pretext for making him come to my house. But does an amorous woman ever lack stratagems for satisfying her passions? Dear reader, this is the one I employed. I shall leave it to your good self to decide whether it was adroit.

One day when Madame Marcelle and Father Hercules were dining with me, I steered the conversation towards the subject of the life one leads in the country. I said that it was necessary to have some manner of occupation in order to avoid boredom, especially in the winter when one was often confined to the house. That, for my part, I could not imagine how a woman could spend the whole year in such pursuits as embroidery, since that occupied only the fingers, leaving the mind in an unbearable state of inactivity.

'For myself,' I said, 'I should prefer to see a lady engaged either in drawing, or painting... or making music.'

'Do you like music then?' enquired Father Hercules.

'Yes, Father,' I replied. 'In fact, it is my passion. I have always desired to learn it but until now my affairs have always prevented me from doing so.'

Madame Marcel told me that she regarded the art of music as very innocent and that she should like to study it with me but now considered herself too old to learn. 'However,' said that good lady, 'you are still young and ought to succeed well in your studies.'

My lover, who was extremely pleased to have an opportunity of giving me pleasure, expressed his agreement with this opinion and said that he should send the monastery organist to me; he was a very good musician and a superior performer upon the pianoforte and had retired to the country with the express purpose of giving more time to his art.

You may easily imagine how agreeable this proposition was to me. What particularly pleased me was the fact that both of my guests had been so completely deceived, and that my lover was himself furnishing the means to render himself a cuckold, without even realising it.

The next day, Father Hercules sent the organist to see me. As you can guess he did not demand an unreasonable sum im payment for his lessons.

Our first eight encounters took place with such an air of cool reserve on my part that anyone other than a musician would have been most disconcerted. In fact my apparent indifference, far from discouraging him, served only to render him more enterprising. At last, he openly declared his passion to me, and intimated that he earnestly desired to give me another kind of lesson which had little to do with music.

When two persons both have the same desire, it is generally not long before they endeavour to satisfy it. We only deferred our satisfaction for the time it took to ensure the most complete secrecy, and then we agreed that the first meeting should take place in my bedroom on a certain night. I was quite sure that since I had not succeeded in giving Father Hercules a stiff prick the previous night, he would not yet be in a fit state to present himself for combat. Yet for fear of a surprise visit on his part, I took care to bolt the garden gate and having thus set my mind at rest was able to turn my whole attention to the joys of love. The long abstention which my monk had been constrained to impose on me filled me with longing for the moment when the organist should arrive.

How slowly time passes when one is waiting! Had I not been forever consulting my watch, I should have imagined that the hour of our tryst had long since passed and that my lover would not be coming. The period of waiting, however, had been as cruel for him as for myself. When at last he arrived, he said that those people who say that time flies can never have had an amorous rendezvous, or they would never say such a thing.

After the preliminary embraces which are usual on such occasions, having only a short time to do that which we wanted to do and not wanting to waste precious mometns, we went to bed ... What a splendid horseman my lover proved himself to be that night! He kept going for two or three hours and made eight prodigious gallops, the first four without quitting the saddle and the four others after very short rests! One may easily guess that in my whole life I have not often encountered such a vigorous athlete. I am even persuaded that had he not been obliged to take his leave of me at such an early hour, and had he been able to arrive sooner, he would easily have completed a dozen! My young organist seemed in no way fatigued by his amorous labours and even begged me to let him begin again. But realising that daybreak was approaching, and fearing besides to reduce him to Father Hercules' state if I were too immoderate in my demands, I refused to accede to his desires. In fact, I pressed him to depart, whereupon he dressed and left.

My new lover had not long taken his leave when I fell asleep, being greatly in need of repose. I must confess that having been accustomed for so long to a much less copious bill of fare, I was extremely fatigued after such a magnificent banquet of sensual delights. My slumber was deep and visited by the most delightful dreams imaginable. It seemed to me that I was still in the arms of my dear organist, that he was exploring my mouth with his tongue while, lower down, his prick was doing its duty. My bottom was moving back and forth with an inconceivable rapidity. I was in fact near to discharging when Madame Marcelle entered my bedchamber somewhat noisily and woke me up.

One would have had to have been in such an agreeable state, experiencing such pleasure as I was feeling then to be able to form some idea of the vexation and ill-humour that this unexpected visit caused me. I controlled myself, however, and more or less managed to conceal my anger. Then the friar appeared, saying that he had called to pay his respects to Madame Marcelle and, finding she was not at home, presumed that she had come to see me. I requested them to pass into another room while I dressed myself.

Madame Marcelle stayed for no more than an hour and then departed, leaving me alone with the friar. As soon as she had gone, he told me that as his beloved prick had been showing some signs of life that morning when he awoke, he had made haste to acquaint me with the news, being persuaded of its giving me the greatest pleasure. He said that we must waste no time but make the most of this newfound vigour. Since I have never known how to resist such an appeal, I immediately consented to try our fortune.

After having felt my buttocks, my breasts and my cunt, the friar made incredible efforts to fulfil the fine promise he had made me, but all to no avail. It was in vain that I did my best to help him; everything we did fatigued us without raising even the ghost of pleasure. At last, seeing that his prick was losing even the slight firmness which at first it had possessed, I persuaded him not to attempt the impossible. In fact, I advised him to rest a week or two, in the hope that that period would suffice to restore his depleted forces.

Dear reader, could you bring yourself to believe that Suzon, who lives only to fuck, would have condemned herself to such a long abstinence had she not been sure to benefit by the monk's absence? Certainly not. I truly believe I should have preferred the risk of killing my faint-hearted fucker rather than consent to being constantly devoured by the ardent fires of unsatisfied passion. My advice, then, was far from being spontaneous. An opportunity to serve my own ends had presented itself and I was not going to let it pass by.

Safe in the knowledge that the friar would not visit me, that he was in no state to show himself to me without embarrassment on his part, I received the music-master every night. If that man did not have the Devil in him, he must have had a ton of spunk in order to support the life we were living. Every day he seemed to become more vigorous. Every day brought new delights: I have never known a man who displayed so much ingenuity in the ways of varying pleasures.

If it were my intention to recount all the different postures that we sampled, I should have enough material to compose a great volume of many pages. I will go further: even those of my readers who are familiar with the celebrated Postures of Aretino[1] have only a feeble idea of all that we did. However, it is not

1. This is a reference to sixteen drawings illustrating the various positions for making love, which inspired the famous Renaissance author, Pietro Aretino, to compose a series of short erotic poems.

my intention to leave this period of my life without describing one of them.

One particular day, after we had proceeded in many different ways, I was quite sure that all the resources of my lover's imagination were exhausted. So imagine my astonishment when I saw him attach the two ends of a piece of cord to the ceiling, thus making a kind of swing. He was careful to arrange the seat of this swing so that it should be at the height of his waist. Since I derived a lot of pleasure from these follies, I always lent myself to them with the utmost good-will. This one appeared to me to be so novel that I watched his preparations very attentively, but I must admit that their purpose escaped me.

When all was ready, he placed me upon the swing, urging me to raise my knees and spread my thighs as far apart as possible, and to make sure that my cunt was thrust well forward. As soon as I was sufficiently instructed in all that I must do, my lover set the swing in motion and stood at a little distance, his prick at the ready. He had prepared everything so well that as soon as the swing was in motion, he did not fail to hit the mark. Giving a thrust of his bum every time, when his prick touched my cunt-lips, he pushed it in as far as possible and caused the swing to move more and more rapidly as our pleasure grew in intensity.

When my lover felt himself to be on the point of discharging, in order not to lose that precious liquor, instead of pushing me away, as he had been doing, the lustful man took my legs under his arms and gripping me firmly by the bum, pulled my belly right up to his and inundated me with a positive deluge of spunk.

This manner of love-making has always greatly

pleased me and I have often repeated it in my life, not only with him but also with various other lovers...

# *The Letters of Eulalie (1785)*

EULALIE IS A COURTESAN WHO HAS LEFT PARIS AND
GONE TO LIVE IN BORDEAUX. THE FOLLOWING
LETTERS WERE WRITTEN TO HER BY HER FRIENDS
AND COLLEAGUES WHO ARE STILL LIVING IN THE
CAPITAL.

Letter from Mademoiselle Julie.

Friday, 17th May, 1782.

My dear friend,

I have been to a pleasure party at the Duke of C's
country seat, at Monceau. There were eight of us in the
company gathered there, four men and four women.
After supper, we all went into a charming boudoir
surrounded by mirrors. Everyone was *in naturalibis* (it
is thus that these gentlemen express the idea of
removing all of one's clothes); then we each chose a
partner and taking up different postures, we all gave
each other the pleasure of watching charming
spectacles. After our amorous frolics, we danced and
did many foolish things until five o'clock in the
morning. Next Thursday we are going to repeat the
performance; how delighted I should be could you but
be there! How everyone would admire your beautiful
body!

Your former maid, who was in the service of that

Urbain woman, has just quit her. She came to see me this morning and told me that since little B . . . has been detained in his regiment by order of the King, there is often not a decent meal to be had in that insolent woman's house. I shall have to see whether I cannot find her a situation with one of my friends. She has charged me to assure you of her respect; she deeply regrets that she is no longer in your service. I must finish: my hairdresser has arrived and I cannot send him away. I am obliged to pay a visit to La Présidente[1] at four o'clock, you will most assuredly guess why. But more of this another time.

Your affectionate friend for life.

Letter from Mademoiselle Julie.

Monday, 20th May, 1782.

My dear friend,

What a strange desire men have! Yesterday, at La Présidente's establishment, I had to spend ages whipping an old government official whilst he, kneeling before me, gamahuched me. Barely had he departed than a young abbé arrived whose inclination was just as singular, although more pleasing. After we had both removed all of our clothes, I had to crawl around the floor on all fours while the abbé followed me in the same manner. When we had done several turns about the room in this fashion, this new Adonis became aroused and took me from the rear, whinnying like a stallion mounting his mare. I was on the point of

---

1. La Présidente was the nickname of one of the most successful procuresses in Paris in the 18th Century. Her real name was Brisseau.

183

bursting into laughter when his instrument, which was long and enormously thick, and which he was pushing back and forth with incredible force, deprived me of the power to do so. At that moment I experienced the most delicious sensations. Twice within a quarter of an hour I felt myself sprayed by the celestial liquor. How happy we should be, dear Eulalie, if all the men who have unusual tastes compensated us for our complaisances with such pleasure as that which my abbé gave me! Thus have I earnestly entreated the Brisseau woman to send for me when he shall come again. I sincerely hope that you may experience such pleasure at Bordeaux. Please write to me frequently.


Letter from Mademoiselle Julie.

Saturday, 25th May, 1782.

A most amusing thing happened at that Lebrun woman's establishment. An extremely elegant gentleman arrived in his coach and asked for a tall blonde woman. Immediately she sent for the Renesson girl. The latter made haste to appear, but imagine her surprise when she recognised her protector, with whom she had been living for a month! Mademoiselle Renesson did not lose countenance however and, immediately adopting a jealous tone of voice, began to heap reproaches upon her lover saying that, having for some time suspected him of infidelity, she had paid someone to follow him. And that, having been instructed of his whereabouts by her emissaries, she had come here to catch him red-handed. Having poured forth a long stream of words reproaching him for his unworthy behaviour and informing him of her

184

bitter grief and disappointment, the hypocritical baggage swept out of the room, forbidding him ever to set foot in her house again. He replied that she need have no fear on that score.

The Lebrun woman was much grieved by this affair and in order to avoid such a thing happening again, is going to have a dormer-window made in such a manner that the young ladies may first see the persons intended for them without themselves being seen.

Always your friend.


Letter from Mademoiselle Julie.

Wednesday, 29th May, 1782.

My dear friend,

What deceivers men are! You know that D... has been my lover for two years and on his account I have refused several protectors, confining myself to brief encounters. Well, I was returning yesterday from my dressmaker and was about to enter my apartment when I heard a noise. Curious to know what it might be, I looked through the keyhole. Heavens! What a sight met my eyes! The infamous D... was about to enjoy my maid who, her bosom uncovered and half lying on my sofa, was defending herself so inadequately that it was easy to see that it was solely to enhance the value of her capitulation. I made a noise at the door, causing them to cease their games and entered the room without saying a word of what I had just witnessed. In the afternoon my maid slipped out of the house without permission, thus giving me a pretext for dismissing her. As for D..., I shall see about giving him his marching orders as soon as a suitable occasion presents itself... if I have the strength to do so, for you know how much he means to me. Never become attached to anyone, my dear, if you wish to make your fortune, and do not follow the example of your unfortunate friend.

Letter from Mademoiselle Julie

Wednesday, 3rd July, 1782.

Yesterday, I dined with Rosette at her invitation. As soon as I arrived, she asked me whether I should not like to earn five louis. I replied that such an offer could hardly be refused. 'Well,' said she, 'this is the way of it –

'Some days ago, an ancient skeleton wearing an immense peruke accosted me at Nicolet's and addressed me thus: "My queen, you are very pretty and I should esteem myself happy to make your acquaintance." I did my best to discourage him but, persecuted by his insistence, I gave him my permission to call upon me. Addressing himself thereupon to my maid, into whose hand he slipped six francs, the ancient beau asked her for my address. Indeed, the very next day my admirer waited on me and showered me with a thousand compliments. Then he offered me ten louis, provided that I should indulge his penchant, which was, he told me, to see two naked women pleasuring each other, adding that I must surely know some young woman who would not refuse to second me. I expressed my willingness to fall in with his wishes and promised to give him satisfaction today at four o'clock. It occurred to me that you might be willing to lend yourself to this piece of foolery.'

'Very gladly,' said I and, the soup being served, we sat down to dine.

Our man arrived at four o'clock precisely. He

greeted us both in the most comical fashion, then wanting to play the gallant a little, he approached us and removed our fichus and handled our breasts. We thanked him for his courtesy and took off our remaining garments. When we were naked, Rosette and I pretended to amuse ourselves. Immediately, the old rake unfastened his breeches, revealing in the broad glare of common day a flaccid priapus which resembled crumpled parchment. Finally, after having rubbed it and shaken it for nigh on two hours, during which time he examined every part of our bodies, covering us with kisses, he managed to make a rather short libation. He praised the beauty and whiteness of our bodies with great enthusiasm and, thanking us for our complaisance, proposed that we should recommence our exertions in one week's time. We accepted, for lack of anything better. Adieu, I must finish for one of my regular visitors has been announced.

Letter from Mademoiselle Felmé.

15th August, 1782.

Last Monday, my sweet, La Présidente requested me to go to her establishment to dine and to spend the night there. Naturally, I complied. Imagine my surprise when I arrived and saw a man of some fifty or, perhaps, fifty-five years dressed like a child of three and who said to La Présidente, 'Mama, is that my new nurse?' 'Yes,' she replied and, turning towards me, she said, 'Here is my son, Mademoiselle, I am confiding him to your care, look after him well. He is a little rascal but all you need to do is to give him a good beating. Here is a cane and a strap, do not spare him. Go into that room with him.' So I went off with my big infant, who it was necessary for me to fustigate for two hours before he managed to make a tiny libation. Afterwards we dined. At one o'clock we went to bed and slept the whole night through. But in the morning we had to repeat the scene of the previous evening. You must agree, my beloved, that the tastes of some men are very *strange*, and impossible to comprehend. One could wish that the celebrated naturalist, Monsieur le Comte de Buffon, might be good enough to give us an explanation.

I am very cross with you because you have not written to me for a long time. Your man of law cannot occupy you to that extent. I imagine that you are not terribly faithful to him. One can easily catch that kind of protector: they are usually as well-regulated as a piece of clockwork. But be careful not to let yourself be caught, as you were with the Marquis de ... Or at least, if it does happen, be well-armed with a convincing story. Never have I known a woman who can put on such a bold face as you, a talent which is essential for women of our condition. Alas! I am unfortunate enough not to possess it: the merest trifle throws me into confusion. Please, my beloved, let me hear from you soon.

Letter from Mademoiselle Rosalie.

19th August, 1782.

This morning at about eleven o'clock, my maid informed me that a young man was asking to speak with me. I desired her to show him into the drawing-room where I joined him after assuring myself that I looked presentable. 'Excuse me for taking the liberty of calling on you without a preliminary introduction,

188

but I have the greatest desire to possess those many charms with which you are endowed. May I dare to hope that you will not refuse me?' At the same time he placed a purse full of gold upon my mantelpiece and positively flew across the room to kiss me passionately and pull me down upon the sofa. Then he set himself to examine every part of my body and to cover me all over with burning kisses.

I was expecting him to take the supreme liberty at any moment and believed that these were only preliminaries, designed to heighten his desires. I tried to help him. But, merciful Heavens! What was my astonishment when I discovered that 'he' was a woman! I became angry, but she threw herself at my feet saying, 'Ah, I beg you, dear Rosalie, do not prevent me from becoming the happiest of mortals.' It was in vain that I endeavoured to resist; the sensations she had aroused in me were too sweet and I was curious to witness the dénouement of this scene. I weakened, she begged me to use my hands for her pleasure and, throwing herself upon me, she thrust her tongue into my love grotto! Ye Gods! With what dexterity did she penetrate every part! My pleasure was inexpressible and several times I filled her mouth with the bitter-sweet nectar of love. As for her, she inundated my hands.

After passing an hour in this pleasant exercise, we paused. We were extremely fatigued: she requested a dish of chocolate. As we sipped the steaming beverage, I expressed my surprise that such a pretty girl should have such an inclination. 'Ah!' returned she, 'if you only knew my history, your surprise would cease.' That piqued my curiosity and I invited her to tell me her story. A little persuasion was necessary but at last she yielded to my insistences and recounted her adventures.

Afterwards she begged me to accord her my favours again. I made no difficulty about consenting. Ah! my dear friend, once more the young lady caused me to experience the most voluptuous pleasures. I must confess, however, that I should not like to indulge too often in such amusements for fear of becoming a tribade. After this second enjoyment, the good lady departed, leaving another five and twenty louis on my mantelpiece. As for me, I took a dish of beef-tea and retired to my bed from which, at seven o'clock in the evening, I have risen in order to recount these pleasant events to my dearest Eulalie.

Letter from Mademoiselle Rosimont.

Paris, 30th August, 1782.

My dear friend,

Last Thursday at Nicolet's I met a German baron who agreed to give me four louis to dine and sleep with him. We had reached the second course, when Victoire came to tell me that someone who was waiting in my antechamber desired to speak with me. It was D..., of the Royal Bodyguard, who had escaped from Versailles to come and spend the night in my arms. I tried to convince him that it was impossible but he would not listen. He announced that he was going to send the baron about his business. 'But,' I replied, 'you may well find that he will not give in without a fight.' I begged him to be reasonable, saying that he would involve me in a scandal; however, it proved impossible to talk any sense into him. I was truly at my wits' end when I hit upon an expedient to which, fortunately, the young man was willing to lend himself. Having first recommended that he should ply our Teuton plentifully with drink, I then presented him to the baron as a relative of mine who had brought me news from my family, and he dined with us. When the baron had become extremely tipsy. I helped him to get into my bed, and ordered that clean sheets should be put in my maid's bed, where I slept with D..., having arranged with her that she should lie with the baron. At six o'clock in the morning D... took his leave. Then my maid and I changed places. As soon as I had laid down beside the baron, I fell into a deep slumber, D... having greatly fatigued me. I did not wake up until eleven o'clock. You may imagine my surprise on finding that the baron was no longer there.

Ashamed of having made a spectacle of himself the previous night, he had risen quietly and quitted the house. Who would have imagined it? He is not like most of his fellow countrymen; that would be a mere trifle to them. I shall remember this episode for a long time. Farewell, my dear friend. You see, as I promised, I never write to you without recounting something worthy of your love of mischief.

P.S. I forgot to tell you about a man who I entertained at La Présidente's establishment who had a peculiar deformation: he had but one ball! Have you ever seen anyone like that? For me it was the first time. He informed me that *that had prevented him from becoming a priest*. Is it not extraordinary? As they are obliged to remain celibate it seems to me that their balls are an encumbrance. In my opinion, they all ought to be castrated. I'll wager that the number of them should then diminish with surprising speed.

Letter from Mademoiselle Felmé.

Paris, 27th September, 1782.

My beloved,

A few days ago something most diverting happened at the Lebrun woman's establishment. The Bishop of . . ., dressed in secular garments had arrived there to indulge in a little dissipation. He had been but a few moments in a private room with a young woman, when a rather brutish man, wanting to have the same girl, and in spite of anything that could be said to dissuade him, went so far as to break down the door of the room where His Lordship had retired with his female companion. Hardly had the two men caught sight of each other they cried out, the one exclaiming, '*You*, abbé!' and the other, '*You*, Your Lordship!' The bishop, trying to assert his authority, said, 'I should never have expected to find *you* here.' But the abbé, visibly unimpressed, replied, 'No reproaches, please, Your Lordship; neither you nor I is in his rightful place. Let us come to an amicable agreement: keep your young lady, I will choose another and then we can all take our pleasure together.' The bishop agreed to the abbé's proposal and they had a merry time. It was in vain, however, that they requested the young ladies to keep the matter secret, for *they* had no greater desire than to render the affair public as soon as possible. Now it is the talk of the town. In fact, because of the scandal, the bishop has retired to his diocese. Farewell, dear heart.

Letter from Mademoiselle Julie.

Friday, 1st November, 1782.

One morning recently, my servant informed me that a woman describing herself as a dealer in second-hand ladies' garments desired to speak with me. I gave my permission for her to enter.

Approaching my bed, the woman expressed a wish to be alone with me. I asked Sophie to withdraw, and she began thus, 'Having seen you with my own eyes, Madame, I can easily understand why the person who has asked me to come and speak in his favour should be so passionately attracted to you. A Russian prince who has seen you several times at the theatre is positively dying to have you at his disposition for a few moments. He will be leaving soon to return to his country and says that, unless you render him happy he really will die. He has charged me to ask what price you put upon your favours and should you not wish to meet him here in your home, then I shall be only too happy to place my modest dwelling at your disposal. I live on a second floor, I sell dresses, so no suspicions will be aroused. The prince will come there and you can both use a room which is at the rear.'

I replied that it was not possible for me to accept this offer as my protector was a most honest man to whom it was my desire to remain faithful. 'Very well, Madame,' she returned, 'but you ought to seize such an excellent opportunity with both hands. They do not often occur. Youth and beauty soon pass and one ought to profit from them and put by sufficient to console oneself when autumn comes. Believe me, Madame, the prince is generous and a man of strong desires, he will give you whatever you want. Your infidelity will be a *sword-thrust in the water* which will leave not the slightest trace.'

At length, persuaded by her reasoning, I told her to inform the prince that if he would be kind enough to give me five hundred louis, I should lend myself to his desires. The woman returned three hours later to acquaint me that the prince had accepted my proposition and that he had even sent two hundred louis for me as an earnest of our agreement. I accepted the money and we settled that I should go to her apartment the next day at nine o'clock in the morning.

I was true to my word. The prince was already there and received me with all the caresses of a passionate lover. As he was anxious to proceed, we went into the aforementioned chamber which had been made ready for us and where, having made me sit down upon a sofa, the prince amused himself for a while by reviewing my charms. Then, suddenly uncovering himself, he displayed a virile member the size of which made me tremble. No, never in my life have I seen a man so strongly constituted! It seemed to me as if everything I had ever seen previously was but a pale shadow of what I was seeing now! My hand could not contain it, and I despaired of his ever being able to make use of such a formidable instrument with me but, laughing delightedly at my astonishment, the bearer of that mighty tool laid me down upon the sofa and set about putting it into the place designed by Mother Nature to receive it.

Only with the expenditure of a great deal of effort did he enter the grove of voluptuous pleasure. But after a few energetic thrusts on his part, my sufferings were speedily transformed into a torrent of delights. As for the prince, he had lost all self-possession, he seemed to exhale his entire soul with his sighs. Four times, without once quitting the place, had he inundated me when I requested that we might rest and compose ourselves. He complied and we partook of some refreshments, then a quarter of an hour after, we recommenced our exertions. I found the prince as animated and as vigorous as the first time. What a man! I have never seen his like, not even the abbé of whom I told you some time ago.[1]

Finally, after three assaults similar to the first, I was forced to beg the prince to cease his vigorous attacks, assuring him that I could do no more, that I was indeed vanquished. He thanked me in the most courteous manner, kissed me many times and gave me the three hundred louis we had agreed upon. Since then I have heard no more of him. Was I not fortunate, my dear friend? As you can see, Fortune and the Pleasures are uniting to render me the happiest of women. Farewell.


Letter from Mademoiselle Rosimont.

                    Paris, 18th November, 1782.
My dear friend,

Two days ago Father Anselme, a Carmelite friar, came to visit me. Never have I been so *well-ridden*. I must admit that until then the idea of giving myself to a monk was repugnant to me, but his manner of approaching me proved to be irresistibly seductive: when he entered my room he placed five louis upon the

---

1. See the letter dated 20th May, 1782.

195

mantelpiece and, displaying a priapus of the greatest proportions to me, he said, 'For fucking with such an instrument one ought not to have to pay, *but the priest has to live off the altar*.' Whereupon he laid me upon my bed, without once detaching himself, he innundated me five times. And perhaps you think that was the end of it? Well, you are mistaken, he resumed his labours and did it three more times. My word, long live the Carmelites! If they are all as vigorous (and Father Anselme assures me that they are) their renown is well-merited. I was truly satisfied with him, as he was with me. He told me that he shall come and visit me again and has even promised to recommend me to one of his friends. Adieu, I hope that you too may find some Carmelites or, at least, men who resemble them.

Letter from Mademoiselle Julie.

Thursday, 2nd January, 1783.

Two days ago I made the acquaintance of a young officer in the Gardes Françaises who cannot be more than seventeen years of age. He has the most handsome features that I have ever seen. Yes, I admit that I am in love with him; I really should like to make him my own and spoil him with lots of presents. It seems obvious to me that he is a novice; how pleasant it would be to give him his first lesson in love! Yet how surprising at that age to be still a virgin; in Paris! I shall soon find out. He is coming to see me tomorrow and as I am positively dying to play my little games with him, I shall give him every encouragement to show me whether he knows very much. Moreover, if necessary, I shall make the first advances, whatever that might cost me.

Love listens to no remonstrances and ignores propriety. As you can see, my dear Eulalie, I am preparing to start the year in fine form. Certainly you may rest assured that I shall not let it pass without trying to obtain my share of happiness. I hope you are keeping well.

Letter from Mademoiselle Julie.

Saturday, 4th January, 1783.

Dear Friend,

Yesterday, my little officer arrived at ten o'clock in the morning, as I had requested him to do. I was still abed. Sophie brought the young man into my chamber and set a chair for him close to my bed. Straight away he seized one of my hands and, covering it with kisses, said that he loved me to the point of adoration, that since seeing me he had not slept a wink, that I was the sole object of his thoughts, a burning fire was consuming him and that should I not return his love, he was likely to die of chagrin.

Alas! his eyes spoke even more eloquently: they were animated by such emotion! His discourse, which he delivered with so much warmth and sincerity, together with the love with which the young man had already inspired in me, was arousing at least as much desire in me as in himself. I caressed the back of his neck, gave him a passionate kiss and told him that a young lady risked a great deal in putting too much confidence in the seductive words of a young man and that inconstancy and indiscretion were the least evils to fear in a tender commerce with men of his age and situation.

'Ah,' he replied, 'I do not know what others are like,

but for myself I swear to be discreet and to love you as long as I live!' Then he kissed me and straight away sank onto my bosom where he lay like one annihilated. He shortly recovered the use of his senses, however, and began to kiss me again, sighing tenderly. I realised then that he was a novice and sighing for something he dared neither take nor ask for.

I rang for Sophie and rose immediately, quite determined not to waste my morning, but to make my pretty boudoir the scene of our frolics. I put on a light quilted déshabillé, my corset was open and my hair hung down in a coquettish disorder. Thus arrayed, I passed into the boudoir with him and, having made him sit beside me on my sofa, I encouraged the young man to possess himself of my bosom and to kiss me as much as he would.

Perceiving that he was in fine mettle, I playfully undid the buttons of his breeches and there appeared before my eyes a wonder which caused me to shiver with both fear and pleasure. Whether by instinct or because my playful manner had rendered him more enterprising, he passed his hand under my skirts and explored there. His features suffused with a pleasing blush, the turbulent state of his spirits and his embarrassment were extreme when, drawing him suddenly on top of me and directing his amorous dart towards the centre of pleasure, I showed him what to do.

I believed then that he would tear me apart, so much did he make me suffer. Several times I begged him to cease, but in vain: like a bolting horse, nothing could stop him. But soon, exhausted by an ample effusion of amorous liquor with which I felt myself inundated, he remained motionless for a moment, as though intoxicated by pleasure. Then, recovering on a sudden from his lethargy, he began in earnest all over again. At last, after four sprinklings, he stopped. As for me, immersed in an ocean of delights, and no longer able to feel anything for having felt too much, I was in a kind of swoon.

My pupil occupied himself with considering my charms and the caresses and the kisses with which he was covering every part of my body restored me to my senses. Overwhelmed with fatigue, I went back to bed. My lover asked whether he could not join me there – a request which I granted, knowing that the Count was at Court, but upon the condition that he should allow me to sleep. He promised to leave me in peace, yet we had been in bed but one short hour when the rogue broke his promise. I would have scolded him if I had had the strength to do so, but that proved impossible. Finally, after another hour of savouring yet more pleasures, we rose and dined together. At four o'clock I sent him away and retired to bed, having great need to restore my depleted energies.

Farewell from your faithful friend.

Letter from Mademoiselle Julie.

Friday, 7th February, 1783.

My dear friend,

You must know that the Marquis de M... had been living with the lovely Sainte-Marie for three months. Suspecting that she was unfaithful to him during the frequent trips which he was obliged to make to the Court, he paid someone to spy upon her. It was reported to him that the Bishop of... often replaced him in the lovely lady's bed. Piqued by this affront, he resolved to take an advantageous revenge. Consequently, he acquainted his mistress that he had to undertake a journey which would necessitate his absence for several days. The prelate, being informed of the absence of the Marquis went, as was his custom, to pay his respects to Mademoiselle Sainte-Marie.

The Marquis came in the middle of the night and, having a key of course, quietly let himself into the house. When he reached the bedside, he drew back the curtains and admirably counterfeited astonishment at finding His Lordship there. 'You are very welcome here,' said he, 'but in truth it is not just that I should pay for your pleasures. This three months past I have been living with Mademoiselle and she has cost me fifteen thousand francs. Now, you must return this sum to me or I shall send for the Watch to have you arrested and taken back to your palace.'

The Bishop tried to come to a compromise, but the Marquis was adamant. He parted with what money he had upon his person and wrote out a bill of exchange for the rest, payable the following day. The Marquis drew the curtains, wishing them a good night and informing His Lordship that he was ceding all his rights to the lovely lady to him. The bill of exchange being duly honoured the next day, the Marquis was in haste to publish his adventure, which is now the talk of the town. His Lordship is more mortified because of it than because of the money he has lost. It is generally believed that he will feel obliged to retire to his diocese for a while.

Letter from Mademoiselle Felmé.

Paris, 3rd June, 1783.

At last, dear heart, I have made up my mind. I shall sell my diamonds and jewels; some of them shall serve to provide me with a life annuity, and I will retire to the provinces. I am tired of the life I have been leading. It is my wish that I should be my own mistress and that if I wish to give myself to someone, advantage should no longer be my guide. Henceforth, love alone shall perform that office. I shall never marry, for fear that my husband might one day take it into his head to reproach me for past misconduct. If some provincial takes my fancy we could live together, but without the sacrament. Those are the best kind of marriages, and the ones which last longest. I know not yet where I shall settle, but in a few days I shall set out for Roye, which is my place of birth. My furniture has been packed away in big boxes and is with a forwarding agent who will send it to where I shall direct him.

My only regret is not being able to embrace you dear Eulalie, before quitting the capital. It is my hope that if you come back, you may be able to spend some time with your friend. I shall write to you again, dear heart, when I am settled.

Letter from Mademoiselle Felmé.

Roye, 20th July, 1783.

Dear heart,

I have settled in this town where I am leading a most tranquil life. I am savouring the pleasure of bringing happiness to my mother and father who, in their declining years, had been reduced to poverty. It would be impossible to describe their joy upon seeing me

201

again. They knew not what had become of me and believed me dead. My mother seemed like to die of pleasure in my arms. How moving were her caresses! I myself was quite overcome. Ah, dear friend, I have never before tasted such pleasures! In fact, I'd not change my lot with that of the great Guimar.[1] I have let it be known that my fortune was won on the lottery, with the result that I am now received in several respectable houses.

I am in disguise as it were and am constantly on my guard against using expressions which would be considered shocking here. It is something of a strain but it will undoubtedly become easier as time passes. If you return to Paris you really must come and see my contentment and the way one lives in the provinces. It is so different from the capital. I sometimes laugh to myself at the affected airs which the sociably inclined of both sexes give themselves.

I have caught the eye of a municipal councillor; it seems to me that he would like me to become Madame Councillor. I have never seen anything like his way of paying court to a lady: he is so measured in all his gestures and all that he says. One would think that he was always making a speech. As you may imagine, he is wasting his time with me.

You know my address now, dearest heart, so I am hoping to hear from you sometimes. As for me, I fear that my letters to you may prove to be rare since it is unlikely that there will be much of interest with which

1. A famous actress of the period who became wealthy and who was much sought after by the richest members of the aristocracy.

to acquaint you. But be assured that I am always your friend.

Letter from Mademoiselle Florival.

Paris, 31st October, 1783.

Dear Pussy,

Mademoiselle Victorine received me with the greatest marks of kindness. She presented me to La Présidente who, yesterday, arranged for me to sup with two Italians. Their passion, though it was quite extraordinary, had nothing unnatural about it however. What they liked was for one of them to get on all fours while I lay on his back so that the other one might fuck me. It was, in truth, a little fatiguing.

It seems to me that my affairs will prosper here. Believe me, my dear Pussy, I shall not forget the service you rendered me in furnishing me with those letters of recommendation. I should so much like to have the opportunity of demonstrating my gratitude to you. Please give my kindest regards to all our acquaintance.

Letter from Mademoiselle Florival.

Paris, 17th November, 1783.

Pussy,

You neglected to tell me that it was necessary for me to register with the Inspector of Police. He sent for me and started to reprimand me but my face pleased him and he took me into his private bureau. I had to give in to his desires in order to secure his protection. As he was passably handsome, it was not so terrible. The Superintendent of the quarter also sent for me but this time it was a much less pleasing experience: he was an ugly skeleton who pawed me for an hour and made me whip him until my arm ached and all that resulted was a discharge of a few miserable drops! Had I dared, I would have told him to go to the Devil. They are right who say that *every profession has its drawbacks.*

I am kept as busy as possible by La Présidente for the Gourdan woman's recent death has resulted in a lot of extra affairs for her. In her establishment I entertained a man who had the oddest desire: first of all I had to rub my derrière with gooseberry jelly, then he knelt between my legs and licked it all off while I was required to play with his chocolate-maker.

They are much less virile here than in Bordeaux. One has continually to apply the birch and the whip, even with young men. I pity the fuckstresses, they can find little to content them here.

Dearest Pussy, I hope to have the felicity of seeing you in six weeks at the latest and then I shall have the pleasure of assuring you of my everlasting attachment.


Letter from Mademoiselle Felmé.

Roye, 22nd November, 1783.

My dear heart,

One can be sure of nothing in this life, vanity has seduced me and tomorrow I shall become the Councillor's wife. In truth, what persuaded me is the fact that my future husband is a fool and I shall be able to twist him about my little finger. By this marriage I shall become related to some of the best families in the town. I will even have the honour of being a second cousin to Monsieur Le Lieutenant General. My wedding is to be a brilliant one: there will be a banquet in the town hall and a ball will be held in the evening.

My change of condition causes me a great deal of quiet laughter. I only wish that you might be among the guests tomorrow; you could not fail to be amused. As for me, I am preparing to be very bored. I shall be quite overwhelmed with civilities and must resign myself to being embraced from morning till evening.

But what vastly amuses me in advance is the thought of the foolishness which I shall be obliged to put on when my husband shall wish to try my supposed virginity. I have taken my precautions and made an ample use of astringent vinegar and chervil, which has been most successful. This morning, I was quite unable to introduce the tip of even my little finger into it. Thus all will appear to be as it ought to be, all the more so as I have remarked that my husband-to-be is well-endowed. But that is not because I have permitted him the least familiarity: I could judge of that by the state of his breeches when my presence inflamed his desires.

I must regretfully break off here, for my fiancé awaits me. Before long, you shall hear all about the wedding, and especially the wedding-night.

Letter from Mademoiselle Florival.

Paris, 7th December, 1783.

Dear Pussy,

Since last I wrote to you, a most unexpected piece of good luck has befallen me. An old man whom I encountered at La Présidente's has taken a particular fancy to me; he has provided me with a small furnished apartment for four months provided that during that period I shall be able to flagellate him whenever he wishes and satisfy his desires by hand. This is all he requires and apart from that I shall be free to employ my time however I will. We shall meet only about three times a week and then only for an hour or two at the most. I am so happy. My previous apartment was extremely expensive.

Please, Pussy, can I so far impose upon your good nature as to ask you to send on the things that I left in Bordeaux? For, you see, I have absolutely made up my mind to settle in Paris. It is quite clear to me that this is the only place where one can make one's fortune in a career of libertinage. Bordeaux is nothing in comparison, and one is so restricted there since the Duke de Richelieu is no longer in command. Yet people ought to realise that we are necessary, and that without us, honest women (if such there are) would no longer be in security. I hope to hear from you soon.

Letter from Mademoiselle Felmé.

Roye, 9th December, 1783.

My dearest heart,

It has been impossible for me to give you an account of the wedding before this since my time has been constantly occupied with parties and visits. All very boring! But I have done my duty now.

On the 23rd of last month, all my husband's relations and mine came to fetch me at ten o'clock in the morning. I was superbly attired for the occasion.

As for the bridegroom, he was wearing his black robe. Everyone was wearing his Sunday best, and there were clothes there which must surely have dated from the time of King Guillemaux and which had not seen the light of day for thirty years.

We entered the church at eleven o'clock. Upon our arrival, all the bells began to ring and the organist grievously maltreated a symphony. After the service, we repaired to the town-hall where we were greeted by a discharge of muskets. We entered a room next to the one where the banquet had been prepared, and I was obliged to abandon my face to everyone. Never have I been kissed so much in all my life! After these compliments, we went in to the wedding-breakfast. They started toasting me during the first course and that continued until we reached the dessert when songs were sung in my honour and once again everyone kissed me. At six o'clock the dancing started, which continued until ten o'clock then a light repast was served, after which I was conducted in triumph to my new home, amidst a thousand jokes about the coming night. As you may well imagine, I was exhausted after such a day and felicitated myself that the end was in sight.

My preparations for bed took an hour; I played the part of the bashful bride to perfection. I was hardly in bed when my new husband came to join me. I hid my head under the clothes and informed him I should not come out until he had extinguished the lights. He begged me most earnestly to keep them alight, but I did not relent until he had complied with my request. Then he began to caress me insistently. I resisted at first, as much as seemed proper, but then yielded and let him take possession of me.

Oh how I groaned then, how I shrieked, how I struggled! In short, I played my part so well that he was more than three hours putting it into me and had he not been exceptionally vigorous, there is little doubt he would not have attained his end that night. Because of my abstinence since leaving Paris, my pleasure was so intense that I was obliged to exercise the most severe control over myself lest I should abandon myself to my senses and run the risk of arousing his suspicions.

In the morning I was aware that my husband had woken up but pretended that I was still sleeping. He cautiously raised the sheets and began to examine my charms. Seeing that they were inundated with blood, he could not prevent himself from exclaiming, 'Ah, my wife was a maiden! How happy I am!' And immediately he began to cover me with kisses.

It was only with the greatest difficulty that I prevented myself from bursting into laughter. But I pretended that he had awakened me and gave a scream, as though shocked to see a man in bed with me. He threw his arms round my neck and overwhelmed me with tender careses. Perhaps that might have led to other things had not someone entered our chamber just then.

You see, dearest, everything is for the best. My husband is all the time boasting of my virtue and publishing abroad my virginity. The next time you are in Paris, you really must come and see the Councillor's wife, who loves you quite as much as when she was just plain Felmé.

# *Memoirs of a Famous Courtesan (1784)*

It is quite common for people to decry pleasures when they can no longer enjoy them. But why distress young people thus? Is it not their turn to frolic and feel the joys of love? Let us then anathematise these as they were in Ancient Greece only to multiply their charm and fecundity. Then the less unreasonable dotards, although prematurely aged, will be supportable and even amiable again. This philosophical idea must be sufficient to give my reader the key to those which I shall soon disclose to him. Thus, without any other preamble, I shall begin my story.

All thinking beings have a favourite penchant which drags them along willy nilly and seems to take precedence over all their other passions. I have mine, like other people: it is the love of pleasure, or to make myself clearer, the love of fucking. That is the cause of all my follies and disorders. These two words compel me to confess to the reader the nature of my profession.

I am a whore, I declare it without false shame. After all, is it such an evil thing? Let us examine the idea. What is whoredom? It is a way of life in which one follows nature without restrictions. After such a clear definition is a whore such a contemptible creature then? What am I saying? Does she not think better than other women? She has a deep understanding of nature and its various ways. Who could be more reasonable? I have said enough, I believe, to establish the excellence of my calling. For the rest, ask no more of me: it would be beyond my capacity to support my statements by grand words and solid logic. I have always detested long sentences. Provided that I can make myself understood, that shall suffice me. Thus I repeat then, I shall begin my story without any preamble.

There was nothing illustrious about my birth: this avowal is not however by any means habitual among women of my condition. I know many of my dear and venerable colleagues who have conferred a fine origin upon themselves, without being any the more noble for it. To hear them speak, it is impossible to wriggle one's bum effectively unless one is the daughter of a prelate, a councillor's niece, or cousin to a duke or peer. What folly such genealogies are! A true whore is interested in absolutely nothing but pleasure. She must despise both her birth and her parents and have no other ambition than that of assuaging her passion and making acquaintances which are both useful and agreeable. Let us come to the facts.

I was born in a village which is at a distance of two leagues from Havre-de-Grâce, where it is well known that there is a college. My father was a wheelwright. As far as education was concerned I was brought up as children always are in the country, that is to say very badly. I should have remained a simple country girl all my life had it not been for my natural talents. There was nothing extraordinary about my childhood, except that from my most tender years it was generally remarked that I had a vivacious manner which proclaimed a lively intelligence. So people in the village had a good opinion of me, and the master wheelwright's daughter was considered to be a good girl. My worthy compatriots often referred to me in those terms.

In spite of that, I did not particularly distinguish myself from the other peasants until I reached the age of sixteen years. Until then, my most serious occupations had been learning to read and write. That was the extent of my knowledge, but I was reasonably good at it in that rustic community. Seeing how rapidly I was growing, my mother and father resolved to put me to work. They thought that I would be able to help them, but I was lazy by nature. It was from this natural inclination to sloth – which is innate in all my kind, let it be said in passing – that I derived so much love for my profession. Being good for nothing in my father's house, he resolved to give me some encouragement by sending me to the town. For a long time I had desired to go to market. It was only at the cost of much domestic upheaval and the shedding of many tears that I obtained this commission.

At last a day came when my father charged me with a basket of butter and eggs to sell at Le Havre. I went there with a lightness of heart which I soon lost when confronted with all those fine town gentlemen. How giddy I was at that time, and how different I am today!

Among the persons upon whom my father had instructed me to call was an old Admiralty official who liked our butter. When I arrived at the house, a young man, the old man's son, saw me and condescended to address himself to me. In fact, he flirted with me the whole time I was there. Of all the fine things he said I only fully understood one, which was a graceful compliment upon my beauty. A woman always has ears for that. Moreover, this young man was something less than handsome: sunken blue eyes, an extremely prominent forehead, a very short nose, a livid complexion and, above all, many of the scars left by smallpox. That is what the first man who uttered amorous words to me looked like. One can easily imagine how little I said in reply: I was far too shy as yet to say much. I had left my tongue at home in my village, which I was missing very much at that moment.

When I left that house, I sold what remained and returned peaceably to my village, without much reflection since I was so inexperienced that all the obliging things which had been said to me did not weigh much with me. When I arrived home, my mother enquired how I had found the town.

'Most displeasing,' I said.

'Why, pray?' asked that good woman.

'Ah,' I replied, 'Those gentlemen made me blush.'

One may judge from this short dialogue how very naive I was. It ended with my saying that I should not go to the town again, but my father would not hear of that and obliged me to return there a few days later.

My task was the same and, as you can imagine, it was necessary for me to call upon the old naval official again. I was very much hoping that the son would not be there, but he was a cunning fellow: suspecting that I should be back the next market-day, he was watching for my appearance. My pretty face attracted him, and my maidenhead, for which he was making plans, attracted him even more. This time I was happier with him than on the previous occasion: he contented himself with staring at me, which made me lower my eyes, so naive was I then. However, I left his house feeling a little more bold and set off gaily for my village. You can picture my surprise when, having barely travelled half a league, I saw the young man coming towards me!

'Do you recognise me then?' said he, taking me in his arms and giving me a kiss.

My response was a most frightful shriek. I tried to disengage myself, but to no avail: he held me fast and said that he adored me, and that all he wanted was a little affection in return. All of his fine words were beyond me but I let him continue with his nonsense. Nevertheless, I derived a certain pleasure from what he was saying. I begged him to leave me however, but he said he would only do so on the condition that he might steal a kiss. It was impossible to deny him. Then he kissed me on the mouth with an inexplicable fire. He continued thus for some time, in spite of my struggles. At last, however, he let me go, leaving me with tears in my eyes.

During the rest of the journey, I reflected on what had just happened to me. The kisses which I had received deeply disturbed me. I knew not how or why but I experienced a secret joy deep within my heart. The very memory of those passionate kisses caused a glowing warmth to spread throughout my being which seemed to concentrate itself in *that noble part of my person* of which, at that time, I knew neither the usage, the charms nor any of the prerogatives, and upon which now and then, as if moved by an involuntary force, I placed my distracted and trembling hand. I pressed it through the veil which covered it in order to try to assuage the longing which was devouring me. I attributed these natural feelings to the young man's attentions and came to the conclusion that these town gentlemen were worth ten of my stupid village lads.

The more I visited the town, the more I was confirmed in this idea. My lover (for I think I can truly name him thus) then made me a thousand tempting offers. He desired to place me in the house of a lady who was a friend of his where, he said, it would be possible to see me very often and where he would give me material proofs of his tender feelings. Bit by bit, I absorbed the poison. Nevertheless, another three months went by before my final capitulation. I continually hesitated. But at last, obsessed by the young man's importunities, tired of living in my father's house, flattered by the hope of future happiness, I resolved to accede to all his desires the next time I should see him.

I did not have long to wait. The next market day, when I went to town, my lover redoubled his instances. My resistance was of short duration, then I gave in. He was overjoyed at the prospect of possessing an object as amiable as myself! His preparations had been made long since and he conducted me without delay to the house of the said friend, who was a dressmaker. It was in a distant quarter of the town and it was there that I abandoned forever my eggs, my butter and my poor basket.

Until now the reader has witnessed my simplicity, one might in truth even say my stupidity. From now on I shall be quite different, for Nature alone shall be my guide. What progress one makes when one follows maxims, precepts as indulgent as hers! The dressmaker's house was the first theatre where I shaped myself in the ways of pleasure: There I undertook my apprenticeship.

I must admit that the house impressed me when I first saw it. My eyes, it is true, were not accustomed to grand spectacles: a simple cottage, a hut with a few sticks of furniture had until then appeared to be beautiful. But when I made the comparison with the apartment my lover was offering me, I was very sensible of the contrast and a great happiness possessed me; the prospect of a brilliant future seduced me to the point where I believed myself to be blessed with eternal happiness.

My lover permitted me sufficient time to admire everything to my heart's content, then came the moment which was to be critical for my virginity. I knew perfectly well why he had brought me to that house, so I did not play the fool nor the prude. Besides, I was not experienced enough for that. Thus my lover placed his hand on my treasure, and fingered it as much as it pleased him to do, and he kissed me repeatedly without encountering any resistance on my part. I made no effort whatsoever to avoid his ardent caresses. But though he did not have to combat my will, yet he had other obstacles to vanquish. He was not of a size readily to ravish a maidenhead: his prick, which was bigger at the top than at the base, would have been excellent for a dowager. For some considerable time, he struggled to enter my plaything, without being able to force open the lips.

My lover had already made several libations, and

very copious ones, upon my thighs, which had not aroused the slightest emotion in me. At that time I did not know the preoccupation every girl and woman has in not losing a single drop of such a precious liquid. At last, after an hour of torment and combat, my champion entered the fort: he had conquered me, but at such an expense of suffering on my part that it seemed impossible to me that I should ever survive such a terrible assault. All the time I had been screaming, shrieking and begging him to desist.

'Is it in this fashion,' I sobbed, 'that you abuse my confidence? Will you not be content until I am dead?'

But no sooner had I uttered these words than a dramatic change occurred in my feelings: time seemed to stand still, my cheeks flushed, a warm glow suffused my body and a sweet intoxication took possession of all my senses. At last, I had been deflowered!

That was the most interesting period of my life. It was that happy time which witnessed the commencement of my pleasures, my chagrins, my joys, my misfortunes. But what am I saying? It was then that I started to live. After my first time everything appeared beautiful to me. Some of my readers may say that I did it too soon. But is it not at sixteen years that one should make one's debut in the world? Had I not done it then, would I at present have so much experience in that variety of pleasures which the public comes to savour in my different nooks and crannies? Undoubtedly no. Let people cease to denigrate what, in my humble opinion, ought to be and has in fact been my greatest happiness, that which has merited the approbation of the finest connoisseurs in these matters, which they have shown by giving me the glorious and flattering title of Nymph of the Day or, in other words: la Dumoncy, fuckstress par excellence.

My reader, seeing me thus separated from my parents, undoubtedly expects me to paint in the most vivid colours their sufferings at having lost me, and also the measures they took to bring me back. In fact, I feel at liberty to dispense with such tiresome details. Let me make myself clear: from the moment I entered the dressmaker's house, my parents no longer meant anything to me and I never heard any news of them. If they occasionally crossed my mind, it was solely pity for their fate that moved me and the hope of one day ameliorating it, thereby paying my tribute to filial piety and by the sentiments of my heart meriting on their part an indulgence for my escapade. But my condition then appeared to me to be much superior to theirs, for I was tranquil and lived without cares, without anxiety, indolent to the point of slothfulness, my sole occupation consisting, to speak plainly, of enjoying the sweet pleasures of amorous dalliance with my lover. Consequently, I did not often venture out into the great world, to avoid being noticed and perhaps obliged to return to my dreary village.

Thus six months passed during which time the only person with whom I had any close communication was my lover. I was most assuredly very virtuous, for a woman must be recognised as such when only one man renders homage to her charms. But that state of affairs did not last long; the moment was approaching when my lover would no longer suffice to satisfy all my desires. After having explored with him all the avenues of love, to the point of exhaustion, it was inevitable that I should have recourse to other men and, unfortunately for him, an excellent opportunity soon presented itself, and I did not fail to avail myself of it. This was the way of it.

A young cavalier, tall and well-built (he was, I believe, a captain of infantry), visited the dressmaker, my hostess, one day on the pretext of placing an order with her. I happened to be present and when he laid eyes on me, the officer addressed me in the most gallant terms, a stratagem for which military gentlemen have a particular talent. Neither did he confine himself to that, but stared at me so intently that I lowered my eyes, being quite unable to sustain such bold looks. That did not discourage him, however; on the contrary, it prompted him to request the dressmaker to go and buy some muslin for wristbands, adding that he had ordered some from a woman whom he named, saying that the dressmaker should bring as much as was necessary and that he would await her return to settle with her. My hostess, being always zealous in the prosecution of business, was only too eager to comply with the gentleman's wishes and she ran off to fetch the muslin, leaving me with the officer.

One may easily guess how embarrased I was! I stood up, went into my room, came back, sat down again and knew not how to keep myself in countenance. Observing my confusion, the officer undoubtedly came to the conclusion that my conquest should not prove to be difficult. He spoke to me in a tone of wheedling flattery for a few moments without being able to draw much response from me. Then, as though we were making a supreme effort to chase away my timidity, he said,

'Look at me, Mademoiselle; please, I beg you!'

I raised my eyes to look at him. But, merciful Heavens! What did I see? Dare I tell? Yes, undoubtedly. For what use would it be for me to affect an untimely bashfulness? After what I have said concerning my situation, it would hardly suit me. Very well then, what I saw was a priapus of the most majestic size. In brief, the biggest and most beautiful prick in the world.

'Oh! Monsieur!' I cried. 'Pray, cover yourself.'

'Very well, O queen of my heart,' said he, 'your wish is my command.'

Then he gave me a hard slap on my buttocks with his left hand, and with his right hand obliged me to lie down on the bed.

'Will you have done, Monsieur?' said I angrily.

'In a trice, my pretty one.'

Whereupon, he took possession of my treasure, caressed it briefly then threaded me with his fine upstanding needle, as though I had been some voluptuous pearl. He moved back and forth furiously, fucking me mercilessly and soon inundated me with a torrent of amorous liquor which filled me with an incomparable voluptuousness. Heavens! What an indefatigable jouster! His priapus, still in form, continued to work hard in order to deserve the homage that my heart and my cunt could not fail to render it. This man had had a great deal of experience with women and knew that it is sometimes good to be a little rough with them. I was happy beyond my wildest dreams. How could it have been otherwise? The spermatic liquor came out in great spurts from my amiable fucker's hot balls and communicated an

219

unspeakable ardour and voluptuousness to every part of my body...! Ye Gods! So much pleasure at one time! Never shall I forget it. I shall remember that gallant officer for the rest of my life...

# *The Adventures of Laura* (1790)

(MADAME DE MERVILLE, THE ABBESS OF A CORRUPT
NUNNERY, IS PLANNING TO INTRODUCE THE SIXTEEN
YEAR OLD LAURA TO THE DELIGHTS OF LESBIAN
LOVE.)

I visited Laura again, determined to risk more this time
than the first. My passion was increasing and so was
my desire! It was clear from what she said that the girl
was as innocent as she was lovely. Quite evidently she
did not understand my ambiguous remarks. A plan
was forming itself in my mind which should not prove
difficult to execute. I left her, and as soon as Brother
Bigprick arrived I acquainted him with my scheme. I
said that his assistance was essential to the success of
my enterprise. His deference to me, which was so often
rewarded, was boundless, and he made no difficulty
about falling in with my plan. I told him then that he
must seek to instruct Laura by questioning her, in the
confessional, upon the matter of impurity; that he
should subtly inculcate her with the desire to read
certain books, actually naming them while appearing
to proscribe them; and that I should be responsible for
the rest. We agreed that the confession would take
place the following day.

What a delightful night I spent in his arms! I

accorded him everything that his lewd passion inspired him to demand of me. Dawn arrived, and we went our separate ways. He promised me to spare no efforts to bring my affair to a successful conclusion and, hoping that I should procure Laura for him after her initiation into our mysteries, he departed feeling happy and satisfied.

I had to attend morning service. How long it seemed to last! 'But nothing that is worth having is ever gained without some difficulty,' I told myself, and bore my suffering patiently. In truth, my dear prior, the public who regard us as vestals are much mistaken. Can they really be so completely unaware that we are women, and that Nature speaks as loudly in our hearts as in those of people whose married state authorises the pleasures they wish to deprive us of? For myself, I do not know why this illusion should prove so enduring. But let us leave this trusting public in its state of naive credulity, for we profit by it. Let us come voluptuously in secrecy and silence, and by our pious mummery continue to hoodwink the people who are only too willing to be deceived.

Bigprick kept his word. After his young penitent had acquainted him that she'd three times lost her temper with the cat, stamped her foot, eaten a pear before going to mass and other childish things which proved the girl's innocence but which she took for great sins, the prior brought the conversation round to the desired subject. It was all Greek to our novice: she did not understand a word! As for me, while Laura was thus engaged, I profited by her absence and entered her cell: there I put that charming novel

222

*Thérèse Philosophe*[1] on her bookshelf. Some expressive plates illustrated this agreeable volume: thus did I hope to pique her curiosity and lead the unsuspecting girl to my ends. I watched for a favourable moment. As that cell adjoined mine, I had made a small opening in the wall. That aperture, of which Laura was of course totally unaware, would enable me to see everything she did when she was alone.

At length, the young lady returned and knelt for a few moments on her prayer-stool. Then up she rose and went across to her bookshelf. The new volume attracted the girl's attention by the freshness of its binding. She opened it and the illustrations immediately caught her attention.

Her cheeks flushed, which seemed to me to be a good sign. She did not know what to think of those diverse postures, then suddenly, realising that this must be one of those books which the confessor had warned her about, she threw it from her with an air of vexation, an action which pained me greatly. The girl remained motionless for a few moments, a prey to conflicting emotions, then the sentiment which I had so artfully inspired in her began to manifest itself.

Curiosity triumphed over piety: she ran across the room and picked up the book. The flush which graced her cheeks 'spoke eloquently of the state of her emotions. She was quite fascinated by the illustrations.

1. *Thérèse Philosophe* was one of the most well-known and widely-read erotic novels in eighteenth century France. There are good reasons for believing that the Marquis de Sade was influenced by it.

The desire to increase her knowledge swept aside Bigprick's hypocritical moralising. She placed a mirror on the floor and put the book on a table. My young pupil wished to verify that Mother Nature had in fact endowed her with the same attractions as those which the women in the plates were making use of.

With trembling hands she raised her skirts and looked into the mirror to see whether she too possessed that centre of pleasure. My dear prior, you may imagine the state in which I found myself at the sight of so many charms! I pressed my eye to the aperture and just a few feet away saw the prettiest mound, the most delightful cunt in the world! Its sealed lips, so rosy and so tender, confirmed its virgin state, a light covering of hair cast a shadow over that charming spot, and the whiteness of her thighs contrasted with the darkness of her pubic hair.

As she made this inspection, her naturally expressive eyes became animated by the fires of passion. If ever a woman has realised the charms with which the poets have endowed Venus, it cannot be doubted that Laura was that woman in those first innocent moments.

The love which was beginning to express itself in her heart, the modesty which seemed to reproach what she was doing established a conflict within her whose effects were extremely seductive. Finally, I could bear it no longer: I left my post for another which promised a thousand delights.

Naturally, I had keys to all of the cells, including Laura's. It was with the greatest stealth that I now opened her door in order to surprise her in the same posture. The application with which she was concentrating both on her own nature, and that represented in the illustrations served me well: I managed to open the door without disturbing the young lady. Then she discovered my presence. You may easily guess how embarrassed she was and visualise her confusion, which was filling me with delight. She lowered her eyes and sought to hide the book. I wished to amuse myself for a moment and expressed an anger I was far from feeling:

'Well now,' I said 'what are you doing, mademoiselle?'

She threw herself at my feet in tears. In truth, at that moment my resistance crumbled: I raised the girl gently to her feet, pulling her against me and placing my hand on a firm breast. I pressed my lips to those of my young charge.

After a brief silence, I said, 'Lovely Laura, the time for play-acting is over. You are of an age when your charms should inspire your happiness. It is my desire to make you aware of what treasures are in your possession, to intoxicate you with the sweetest of pleasures.'

I conducted her to the bed and pressed her down upon it. She was too astonished, too troubled to think of resisting. I covered the dear girl with kisses while my hands eagerly sought out her holy charms. When she felt me raising her skirt, she put up some slight resistance, whereupon I said, 'Divine Laura, until now you have been unaware of the transports which love inspires. It is my desire to introduce you to such delights: you are beholden to love for your beauty and cannot resist its delights. What I am saying surprises you, no doubt, but Mother Nature never loses her rights. We are women and subject to the most tumultuous passions. Give yourself over to those pleasures whose existence you have hitherto been aware of but from which you will derive the greatest happiness.'

Even while I was speaking, my fingers were busily engaged in exploring the most adorable little cunt. I tried to push one of them right in but Laura's protests and cries of pain reminded me that I must have a care since this was a virginal flower; therefore I contented myself with gently rubbing that plump little mound, which gave inexpressible pleasure to my young conquest.

She abandoned herself to me entirely. We gradually revealed our bodies to each other. I repeatedly kissed and caressed her perfectly formed breasts which were as white as alabaster. Her nipples seemed to my eyes to be as pink and delicate as rosebuds. Every part of her received my homage. Her snowy buttocks were firm to my touch. I placed her hand on my cunt, and an agile finger set my senses on fire. I said, 'You will observe dearest Laura, that you do not meet with the same obstacle in me as within yourself. That is an enigma which our prior will resolve for you.'

Oh, how ingenious is love! That gentle virgin masturbated me delightfully! Two hours did we spend, and more, in those delightful pastimes. We each succumbed in turn to the excess of pleasure. When we had recovered our lucidity, she asked me several questions and ran to fetch her volume of *Thérèse Philosophe*. We turned the pages together, pausing when we came to the illustrations. The virile member seemed particularly to draw her attention. I told the lovely girl that it was popularly known as a prick.

I pointed out the two little globes which hung down below the generative organ, telling her that they were enclosed in thick flesh, that these globes were called 'testicles' in surgical terms, and 'balls' in the vulgar tongue. I said that these balls were full of a seed which served for the propagation of the human species. I also told her that the sudden shuddering which overcame both of us when we were touching one another was also produced by the motion of that fluid, which took violent possession of all our faculties and whose emission plunged us into the state of voluptuous exhaustion that she had just experienced.

I spoke to her of the manner in which men and women complement each other, saying that Nature, desirous all the time to be uniting these two different creatures, had distributed her favours equally between them: the one possessing the miraculous tool of our existence, the other the pleasing cavern which so delightfully encloses the productive staff.

Laura asked me the following question: 'But how can that member enter such a tiny nook? It appears to be bigger than a finger and when you tried to put yours inside me it hurt me most dreadfully.'

'Ah, Laura!' I cried, 'how ignorant you are and how delighted I am to have such agreeable lessons to teach you! You must know then that the Creator has made these pleasures, of which I am the apostle, the most exquisite of all. I sing of their delights with both joy and gratitude. Your present state, my child, is one of innocence. You still possess what is known as your maidenhead. It is a precious favour which Nature reserves for a man and of the enjoyment of which you cannot deprive him. A certain amount of suffering is

227

inevitable but will be succeeded by the keenest of pleasure. Those which we have just experienced are only a foretaste of those that you are destined to feel. You have seen that your finger entered without any difficulty into *my* nook. Well, that is the consequence of the sacrifice of which I have been speaking. I used to be as you are now, but an amiable man skilfully ravished my flower and rendered me capable of coupling with my fellow human beings.'

'What is this? A man has caressed you as I have done?'

'Most assuredly. Brother Bigprick does so every night. And I intend to recompense his tenderness for me by helping him to pluck the sweet flower of your virginity. As you will observe, jealousy is not one of my vices.'

'What! A man ... with me? I cannot even think of such a thing without blushing ...'

'What nonsense! In this world excessive modesty only serves to frustrate us of the sweetest advantages. We were born for pleasure. My dear young friend, pray let yourself be guided by me and one day you will realise how much I have done for you. In this cloister we may fearlessly give ourselves over to all the joys of love. For us, inquisitive busybodies do not hold the terror that they do for those who live in society. This evening I desire you to be present at one of our orgies which, as I shall inform our sisters, will start at eight o'clock. The chapter-house shall be prepared for that purpose, for I desire that your maidenhead should be sacrificed with pomp and ceremony ...'

Laura interrupted me, begging me most earnestly not to carry out my plan, saying that it would be impossible for her to appear thus before all her companions, that she would gladly do with me in private what we had already done, but that in public she should never have the courage. I reassured the poor girl by taking her into my arms again and overwhelming her with caresses to which she responded ardently.

I spoke no more to her about my project but instead concentrated upon putting it into execution. It was time for the evening service. We made our ablutions and adjusted our clothing then, carrying our prayer-books, our hands crossed upon our bosoms, eyes fixed humbly on the floor, we went to fulfil our duties.

A nasal and lugubrious chanting led the congregation to believe that we worshipped only one divintiy and that the very name of love was forever banished from that place.

I shall not conceal from you the fact that the celebration which I was preparing for the evening occupied my mind throughout the service. Frequent distractions acquainted the nuns with my state of preoccupation. When the service was at an end, I assembled them together and confided my project to them. Preparations speedily got under way.

I summoned Bigprick to my private quarters and addressed him thus, in a noble tone:

'Venerable fucker, your docile sweetheart wishes to prove how grateful she is to you. Come to our gathering tonight, come and savour the most splendid of triumphs. Come, I want to place Laura's arms around you. Her virginity is reserved for you; I desire to offer you an amorous combat worthy of such an athlete as yourself.'

At these words, his eyes sparkled, his cheeks flushed a deep red. He could only stammer, so great was his joy . . .

'What! Shall I hold such a ravishing creature in my arms? Shall *my* prick have the honour of such a maidenhead? . . . Can it be true? Or am I being deceived by some sweet dream?'

'No, my dear prior. No, you are not dreaming.' While affirming to him the reality of our conversation, my hand had disappeared under his robe and was seeking the sword of sacrifice . . . He understood at once what I required and threw me down upon my bed. You may imagine how well I did my duty and with what energy I moved my arse!

'I am satisfied,' I cried. 'You can see by the sacrifice I'm making that jealousy has no power over me. You know that I have always tried to be just in every way and have never wished to deprive my sisters of the joys which you have caused me to experience. This is the first time I have been able to procure a maidenhead for you and I have seized the opportunity with the greatest pleasure. Your triumph will please me prodigiously; we shall fan the flames of your ardour with fortifying drinks. But I cannot stay here with you any longer, for I must supervise the arrangements which will culminate in your victory.'

I did indeed go then and verify that all was being made ready. The most harmonious symmetry was what guided us, and we waited impatiently for the happy moment to arrive.

A repast arranged with taste and delicacy was to precede our delightful orgy. Excellent wines were on hand to increase our pleasure and I swear that not even the most aristocratic of libertines, not excepting d'Artois and d'Orléans[1], could have conceived of anything better. I left the good sisters to put the finishing touches to the preparations and went to fetch my amiable recluse.

I found her deep in reflection, *Thérèse Philosophe* lying open beside her. Laura's fascination with the novel seemed to me to bode well for our enterprise: the charming style of the lovable storyteller assured me in advance of the young lady's entire submissiveness to my desires. I did not mention my project. We chatted about *Thérèse*, and I made a few observations which further enlightened her. It seemed to me that her personality, which was predisposed towards the liveliest passions, would make little resistance to Bigprick's passionate advances and that afterwards our novice would become the most enthusiastic of hussies.

At last the longed-for moment arrived and I conducted Laura to the room where the banquet had been prepared. By now her fears were causing her some reluctance and so I told her Bigprick would be terribly disappointed if she refused to participate in the ceremony.

'Soon,' I said, 'you will fall under his spell. You are at an age when love speaks loudly in a girl's heart. However, if you wish to consider the matter a little longer, nobody will try to force you. But at least come and grace our gathering with your presence.'

1. The Count d'Artois and the Duke d'Orléans were both members of the French royal family.

At last I persuaded her. The company was already assembled.

Laura stopped short when she saw how elegantly the great hall had been decorated. A table, set with exquisite taste, cried out for the guests to be seated. The gentle light of the candles inspired our hearts with voluptuousness. Before us was the sofa which was to be the throne upon which Bigprick would soon triumph. When Laura arrived, she was surrounded by the sisters who all wanted to kiss her. Ah, my dear Hercules, how you would have enjoyed such a spectacle!... Your imagination must supply the deficiency of my description: see the lovely girl advancing with a timid and hesitant step, see the fires of love in her rosy lips, mingling with the blushes of innocence, see those great dark eyes modestly lowered beneath ebony eyebrows delicately arching on the ivory smoothness of a forehead, see round breasts, fashioned by the Graces, which are clearly discernible through the light wimple, straining against the cloth as though they wished to escape from their prison!

What mortal could remain insensible to the sight of so many charms? Bigprick was deeply impressed. I saw him make a gesture of surprise and, at the same time, his countenance lit up and he could not take his eyes off the young woman. None of us felt jealous, for we owed him too much to begrudge him this moment of enjoyment and, besides, we were certain that he would be grateful for our consideration and would reward us later on.

We all sat down. I had seen to it that Laura was seated between the prior and myself.

I addressed her thus, 'Dear child, you did not expect

to find such a sumptuously laden table in a convent. But you must know that we are extremely rich, that kings, queens and other imbeciles have made considerable donations to us. And we find ways to dissipate our revenue. Meals offer us endless resources and our dear prior is most accomplished in that sphere. He has already written two big treatises on the art of cooking: there is not a bishop who does not possess these nourishing works and who does not exhort his cook to consult them, to meditate upon these books which are more precious than a Holy Decree as far as they are concerned.'

The prior smiled at me and said, 'Dear lady, I shall become prodigiously vain if you continue to flatter me thus. But I know my true worth and I shall not let my head be turned by praise which I do not merit.'

Laura listened, ate, but said not a word. I had made sure that a drink which provokes amorous feelings was prepared and placed before her. Indeed, when she had drunk just a small glass of that philtre, her eyes began to sparkle, Nature repulsed shame, and we prepared ourselves to watch the most voluptuous spectacle.

The conversation became more animated, and words led to deeds. Sister Ursula, who was sitting next to me, kissed me passionately and our mouths remained positively glued to each other for some moments. Our tongues met and soon the whole company was similarly engaged. Bigprick audaciously placed his hand on one of Laura's breasts. The latter's first impulse was to push him away, but soon the example of her companions, and the philtre she had drunk, weakened her resistance to the vigorous prior's urgent caresses.

Sister Saint-Ange came to the aid of the prior and withdrew the pins which held the young lady's wimple in place. Then the most beautiful breasts were offered to our gaze: they were roses and lilies. Their precipitate movement clearly indicated the state in which our maiden found herself. Bigprick, who was impatient to come, had already exposed his long and vigorous member whose proud, rubicund head seemed to menace all the cunts assembled there.

Laura was led over to the sofa and placed upon it. We all surrounded her, covering her with kisses, and unfastened the young lady's clothing. Soon she was clad in nothing but her chemise. She did not utter a word, she blushed and her hands could not find the strength to repulse ours. We handed over the tender, almost naked victim to the great sacrificer.

Ah, my dear prior! What charms! What buttocks! What thighs! Bigprick hastily removed his garments and seized the trembling Laura in his arms. With one hand he pulled her chemise up to her waist, whilst with the other he presented his redoubtable cutlass to the entrance of her sanctuary. The poor girl screamed loudly. He stopped. I caressed Laura, persuading her that it was necessary to suffer a little, assuring her that it was an essential preliminary if ever she were to attain true bliss.

The prior tried thrice more, and thrice was he repelled. But he had managed to lodge the head of his prick ... he did not intend to lose that advantage: he gave such a vigorous thrust of the bum that he entered entirely. A piercing scream from the victim announced the triumph of the reverend brother. He held fast, however, and Laura became calmer. In fact, that young hussy was beginning to enjoy the proceedings and was in truth wriggling her bottom as I might have done. They both reached the supreme moment of delight together.

As for the rest of us, we could not be content to remain mere spectators any longer. Sister Ursula and I threw ourselves down on one of the mattresses which had been placed on the floor in accordance with my instructions. The others followed our example and soon one could see nothing but cunts, bums and breasts wherever one looked. After this pleasant exercise, we gave a dish of steaming broth to the happy couple, and a glass of excellent Cyprus wine.

I kissed Laura, who wanted to get dressed but I prevented her from so doing, telling her that Bigprick would never be content with just one bout. I made her change the chemise she was wearing as it was blood-stained. She wiped herself clean and remained in that agreeable disorder. I engaged the rest of the company to do the like and they applauded my suggestion. In less than no time all of our clothes were removed. Bigprick did the same and we seated ourselves at the table again.

It would be impossible for me to describe to you all the follies to which we abandoned ourselves. Laura was ravishing and was the prime mover of our passions. We all drank beyond the bounds of moderation. I intoned an ode to Priapus to which everyone contributed. At each strophe, every lady present kissed whoever was sitting next to her. Partly naked as we were, we rejoiced in the sight of our half-revealed charms, and to each of them paid a tribute of kisses and caresses.

By now we had moved the sofa nearer to the table. Bigprick and Laura were seated upon it with me by their side and Sister Ursula and Sister Saint-Ange were seated on either side of us. The prior pushed his young bride down on to her back, placed her legs on his shoulders, and endeavoured to bugger her.

'Ah, two maidenheads in one day is going too far!' I exclaimed.

He obeyed me, and directed his attentions to the young lady's cunt. Laura became violently agitated and seconded her fucker's efforts to the utmost limits of her ability.

As for the rest of us, we masturbated each other, since this was our only resource, but we went to it with such a will that we were like to swoon from joy. When this bout was over, we returned to our wine and our songs. Bigprick quoted almost all of Jean-Jacques Rousseau's epigrams to us. It was not long before the conversation, the liquor, and the naked women all conspired to renew his vigour, and he displayed a prick whose length and rigidity thrilled us all. Laura regarded it longingly but, addressing herself to the prior, said, 'It is not fair that I should be the only one to be so pleased today, and the Mother Superior deserves a reward for all her trouble.'

I did not wish to prove myself unequal to Laura in generosity, and told her that since this was her special day she should finish it. She raised more objections. Then I proposed another expedient: 'Very well,' said I, 'let us draw lots.'

Everyone agreed to this suggestion. I was the winner and hastened to lie down on the sofa. But I wanted Laura to participate in my pleasure: I took her in my arms.

I displayed a posterior to Bigprick which I well knew would tempt him. And I was right: he trussed up my chemise and buried his instrument in me. I masturbated Laura and Sister Ursula tickled the brother's testicles.

Never, no never, have I experienced so much enjoyment as fell to my lot that night: we passed it in voluptuous delights.

Daylight began to appear, it was now necessary to attend Matins. In truth, how well disposed we were to perform that office! So, after a brief hesitation, I took upon myself the responsibility of a general dispensation and we carried on with our orgy. Brother Bigprick rubbed all the sisters one after another, and still had enough strength left to shaft Sister Ursula and Sister Saint-Ange. He promised to make it up to the others later on, not wishing to excite their jealousy.

I said to him, 'You must be a very happy man after such a night, but do not count upon your new wife. Do as you will with the others, but I am taking charge of this young lady now. In a few days you may have her again, but before then you must fulfil your obligations and fuck the rest of us.'

As I finished speaking, I clasped Laura to me and could not resist caressing one of her firm breasts. I left off fondling her breast only to stroke her pretty mound. How well she responded to my caresses! And what pleasures her supple and ingenious finger induced in me!

For more than an hour we remained together on the sofa, locked in a tight embrace, gently rocking each other. Our tongues had no more strength. We were positively intoxicated with love. Our eyes closed and we remained in that state of utter prostration for so considerable a time that upon awakening, we found ourselves alone: the others had retired to their cells to seek some rest. We followed their example. I found Brother Bigprick sleeping soundly in Sister Ursula's arms. Their position convinced me that they had fallen asleep after intercourse had taken place.

'Come,' said I, 'we must not disturb them. Let us go to bed.'

I closed the door softly and we entered my quarters. We got into bed. I wished my young companion a good night and slept for about two hours. When I awoke, it was broad daylight. I made Laura get up. I went into all the cells and found everyone still sleeping. I told them that they must go to morning service, so they got dressed.

Bigprick and Sister Ursula were still in the same position and an idea came to me. I gently pulled back the bedclothes and revealed the naked lovers. Then I started to masturbate Bigprick. He did not awake but behaved exactly as men do when they are having voluptuous dreams. However, at the moment of ejaculation he stretched out his arms, I moved forward, he embraced me, and my touch awoke him. He opened his eyes. Imagine his surprise when he found me in his arms!

'Time to get up,' said I.

He obeyed at once and leaped out of bed. I desired to wake Sister Ursula in the same manner and succeeded marvellously. I gently introduced my finger into her cunt and titillated the clitoris. If only you could have seen how she flung herself about, how she

238

moved her bum! She made the bed creak. Bigprick was laughing heartily. However, when she was satisfied, she opened her eyes and said, 'Where am I? What! In your arms!'

'Yes, yes,' said I. 'Come along, Madame libertine, get up; it is time for morning service.'

Bigprick said, 'Good. You go to the service but, as for me, it is impossible to leave at this hour. I shall return to the chapter-house: the remains of last night's feast shall provide me with a breakfast. After the service, you can come and join me there. Still, if you will take my advice, you will each have a little glass of something... to give you the strength to do all that praying and hymn-singing.'

We followed his advice. We went away and each took a glass of orange-water before going to perform our duties.

*(Later that day Laura participates in another orgy and during the following week the young woman takes part in a great deal of such activities with the inevitable consequence that she becomes pregnant. Unbeknown to the Abbess, she also meets a young gentleman when he is visiting the convent, falls in love with him and agrees to run away with him.*

*One day, Madame de Merville finds that her charge has disappeared but soon after receives the following letter:)*

'My dear abbess,

Your lessons, your example have awakened desires within me which it is not in my power to deny. Far from reproaching you, I must thank you for having enlightened me, and if I have a regret it is that of not having become acquainted with you two years earlier, for then those years should not have been wasted in a culpable inactivity. Nature tells me at every moment that I was born for pleasure, and I should not wish to be deaf to a voice which is so much in accordance with my interests.

'Undoubtedly, you will think me guilty of the basest ingratitude for departing in this manner after all that you have done for me. I am aware that your reproaches are not without foundation, but you must believe that never shall I forget you. Here are the facts concerning my flight: Floridor came to the parlour with my parents, as you know; I saw him and was consumed with the ardent fires of love. Bigprick's caresses were only agreeable to me inasmuch as I imagined that they were Floridor's. It was not long before the latter, enamoured of my charms, expressed his passion for me. He bribed one of the sisters to deliver his letters to me. We agreed upon a day when I should flee with him and he brought his post-chaise to the new garden-door, I got into it and we sped away toward Paris. I bore in mind that I had a role to play and had a care not to let him see how much pleasure was mine at being in his arms.

'However, he caressed me a little in the chaise, and I pretended to resist. At last, after he had promised to marry me twenty times, I relented somewhat. We had just arrived at a delightful meadow. I perceived an arbour which decided me. We got out of the chaise. He led his horse close to the arbour, attached him to a tree, and we found ourselves under a sweet-smelling vault of leaves. This spot, which was shaded by hawthorn

240

bushes and at a good distance from the road, facilitated our desires.

'He put his arms around me and drew me to his bosom. Again I played the coy maiden. One of his hands slipped under my skirts, I squeezed my thighs tightly together. At last, after a struggle of several minutes' duration, I contrived to fall. He profited from this circumstance and, pulling up my skirts, he proceeded to have intercourse with me. I struggled, I screamed; by my play-acting I made him believe that he had triumphed over my maidenhead. I appeared abashed, my eyes were lowered modestly, my bosom palpitated rapidly. In order to make my part seem more convincing, I even managed to shed a few tears. He hastened to dry them and, after many protestations of eternal love on his part, we got back into the chaise and continued our journey to Paris. It took us two days to complete the trip. When we reached the first town, I changed my clothes, for that was my first opportunity to do so, so precipitate had been our departure.

'When we arrived at Paris, we took rooms at the Hôtel de Tours in the Rue des Petits-Champs. A great deal more attentions and promises on his part were necessary before I would agree to share his bed, but at last I relented. We passed a delightful night together, and I abandoned myself to all the fire of my temperament. I have now spent two days in such delightful pastimes, but I have made time to write and acquaint you with what has happened so that you should not worry unduly. I can imagine your embarrassment with regard to my parents, but all will be well now, for I have written a letter to them;

however, since it would be foolish to let them know my real whereabouts, I have inscribed an address in Brussels on my letter in order to mislead them. I have charged someone who is instantly departing for that city to send it from that place.

'Adieu, my dear abbess. It is time for me to go to the Opera. I shall write to you frequently, please do the same for me. I kiss you all with the tenderness of both a friend and a lover.

Laura de Fondeville
Paris, 20th November, 1790.'

I summoned the whole community and acquainted them with this letter, at the same time revealing my fears to them... fears which proved to be only too well-founded.

'This Floridor,' I said, 'appears to me to be a libertine, and I greatly fear that Laura has been duped by him. But one cannot avoid these first skirmishes in love. Had she consulted me, I should have advised the young lady to repress a passion which might prove to be dangerous. She lacked for nothing here, and this precipitate flight shows just how inconsiderate and thoughtless young people can be. She is only sixteen years of age. She might have savoured all the pleasures here for some years. During that time, her parents would have found a suitable match for her. She would have gone back to them with honour, and would have left the wimple for the bridal wreath: we have the means to repair broken maidenheads and the young lady's husband would have believed his new wife to be intact and pure. But what will become of her now? She is with child. As soon as Floridor becomes aware of that he will abandon her. Ah!' I continued, addressing myself to Sister Ursula, 'you conducted yourself far more prudently. You followed my advice and have profited by it. Your dear mother has arranged a most desirable marriage for you with a rich government official. You will pass from the embraces of Bigprick and myself to those of a husband who will believe that he is teaching you a game at which, in fact, you are already an expert.

'A few drops of our special medicine will soon make good all the ravages which the prior's weapon has made.'

Laura's disappearance affected me greatly, for I had become attached to her. However, I consoled myself to the best of my ability with Bigprick and my nuns: we continued our orgies. A month passed without any news from Laura. Her parents wrote to me saying how upset they were by their daughter's behaviour. I pitied them, and consoled them as well as I could.

Then, after an interval of about six weeks, a letter arrived from our fugitive. Here it is, faithfully transcribed for your benefit:

'Ah, my dear abbess, how foolishly I have behaved! I have been duped by my trust and my love! Floridor, who seemed to love me so much, is nothing but a monster. You know that a casket of jewels which were of great value was in my possession, well the scoundrel has made off with it leaving me with nothing but fifteen francs. You can picture my despair! Fortunately, I had already made the acquaintance of a distinguished gentleman, who is our neighbour. I did not hesitate to acquaint him with my misfortune and my lover's perfidious conduct. He sympathised with my situation and offered me pecuniary assistance.

"You shall be avenged," he assured me, "for the woman with whom he has departed has the most evil reputation and I wager he'll soon have good reason to repent his misdeed. But have a care lest he return and seduce you again, for then you would share his wretched fate. Let us leave this house."

'And indeed, that very same evening we removed to the Chausée d'Antin. I have nothing but praise for this gentleman's behaviour. Quite evidently, it is not his intention to deceive me.

'He said, "I can only remain in the capital for three more months, I cannot take you with me, but before my departure I want to reassure myself that you are provided for. You have a good voice and can read music. I know the director of the Opera and I shall use my influence to obtain an interview for you."

'Indeed, he spoke about me to his friend, who sent for me, listened to my singing and was satisfied with my voice. It was easy to see that I had made an impression upon him. He promised to give me some lessons and added, "I am sure that we can do something for you, mademoiselle. In less than two months you will be ready to join the chorus. Work hard and you will soon be earning money, you have a great deal of talent."

'He wanted me to visit him the next morning at ten o'clock. I promised him that I should keep our appointment punctually.

'I was true to my word. He had had a light meal prepared for us. He showed me into an elegant and ornate boudoir where we sat on a sofa. As you can guess, *Monsieur le directeur* wanted a reward for his protection. I made a show of resisting, as etiquette demands, but soon surrendered to his desires. The director, having no doubt of his triumph, had attired himself for combat: a voluminous dressing-robe enveloped him. But when he opened it, I perceived an extremely fine member thrusting against his shirt, which was all that covered it, for he was not wearing breeches. He grasped my hand and conducted it to that formidable engine. With his free hand he removed my *fichu*. He went into ecstasies at the sight of my breasts, which he found to be admirably white and firm. All the time my fingers were voluptuously squeezing his balls and he did not have time to throw me down upon the sofa, for he suddenly discharged.

'"Ah!" he exclaimed, "the next time we shall not waste time on preliminaries, but get straight to the point."

'He ordered his servant not to let any one enter, and the lesson he gave me had nothing whatsoever to do with sharps or flats, you may be sure. I removed my *fichu* completely and let him kiss and squeeze my breasts to his heart's content. We ate and drank, seated together on the sofa. I placed a little stool under my feet and trussed my skirts up to my knees. He admired my slender legs and his hand caressed my thighs, which he said were beautiful.

"My lover was determined to make love to me properly this time and he pressed me down upon the sofa, which was surrounded by mirrors. I regarded my reflected charms with pleasure and sought, by adopting a more lascivious posture, to render myself more desirable to my lover. At first the size of his prick

245

caused me some discomfort, but that was soon transformed into a positive flood of joy in which we both drowned.

'After his ejaculation, the young man remained prostrate for a while and I endeavoured to restore his vigour. His prick was still lodged in my grotto and I could feel its power gradually returning. I invented a thousand little tricks to arouse him, nibbling, pinching and sucking his chest with my hot lips and my tongue seeking that of my lover. At last my efforts were rewarded and I felt my cunt filled once more with a powerful and vigorous prick. This time he put my legs on his shoulders and slapped and pinched my bottom with both of his hands. We came again and for two whole hours lay there annihilated.

'When I had recovered somewhat, I kissed him. I drank a glass of wine, then dressed myself, not without once more rousing my new lover. But this time I only wanted to kiss him.

'His prick was still bold and menacing and he said, "See the effect your charms have upon me, my pretty. Will you leave me thus without coming to my aid?"

'As he was speaking he guided my hand to his fearful tool. I am good-natured, I let myself be persuaded: I masturbated him delicately with one hand, while with the other I slapped his enormous buttocks. This time he was slow to discharge.

'When he had done so, I said, "You ought to be satisfied now; pray ask no more of me for I must take my leave."

'Then he showed me out by way of a little concealed stairway. I took a carriage and returned to my gentleman.

'The moment he set eyes upon me he began to laugh, staring at me all the while. I guessed the cause of his merriment, and blushed in spite of myself.

'He said, "You have been a very long time, Laura. The lesson would appear to have been an extremely strenuous one."

'"Yes," said I, "the piece was very pretty, and we played it several times."

'"Very good... Listen, Laura: I am not at all plagued by jealousy; you are at an age when the senses are violent. I know my friend: he is amorous and insistent. You were unable to resist him, admit it to me sincerely."

'"In faith, since you desire to know the truth, I shall not attempt to conceal it. I am naturally inclined to be frank and prefer not to dissimulate."

'And so I recounted to him the voluptuous scenes with which I have already acquainted you.

'"Very good, very good," said he, conducting my hand into his breeches. "Your naivety affords me the greatest pleasure and I would like us to repeat such a charming performance together."

'I could not refuse my favours to such an adorable man, especially as I was so indebted to him for his kindness to me. We went into his bedroom. He fetched a bottle of wine, drew the curtains to render the setting more mysterious and, after a small libation in honour of Bacchus, we turned our attention to love. I did exactly what I had done with the director: I removed my *fichu* and raised my skirts to my knees: In short, we followed the same path and experienced the self-same pleasures. However, when I endeavoured to reanimate his forces after the first act of intercourse, I did not find the same resources and we were obliged to let matters rest.

'"Lovely Laura," said he, "you are fertile in expedients, but you do not as yet possess sufficient power to combat exhausted Nature. I came well. I am no longer young and you cannot hope to experience the same pleasures with me as you have with my friend, who is less advanced in years than myself. Your age, your ardent temperament, demand vigorous attentions and, to be frank, with me you will only experience a pale shadow of the pleasures to which you are entitled. All I desire is that, although you may honour a more worthy object with your favours, you should continue to do the same for me. When it is necessary for me to leave Paris, I shall carry with me the memory of the sweet moments we have passed together."

'I could only respond by caresses to this speech which was at once frank and endearing.

'"The moment when we are forced to part will be a very painful one for me," I said. "I have the greatest affection for you. Your honesty has won my esteem."

'The next morning, he was quite insistent that I should keep my appointment with the director. The anticipation of pleasure lent me wings. This time, however, we went into his music-room where I had a proper lesson. When that was finished, we resumed our little games. I was quite enchanted by the new fashions of making love in which he instructed me.

'He showed me a new book of pictures dealing with the matter and said, "We must try all of them."

'Indeed not a day passed without him demonstrating how carefully he had studied the volume. We found some delightful ideas. It is my intention to send you this useful and important book. However I perceive that what started as a letter is turning into a positive treatise; nevertheless, encouraged by your last letter in which you requested me to conceal nothing from you, it is with the greatest pleasure that I am contributing to our correspondence. But if I am going to recount all my follies, you must tell me of yours with Bigprick, to whom by the way I send my affectionate greetings, as well as to your charming companions. Assure them that I shall always be, both for them and for you,

   The tenderest of friends.
                    Laura de Fondeville.'

*(Several weeks pass. Bigprick dies and is replaced by Father Ignatius. Laura appears at the Opera where she meets many admirers and becomes more and more promiscuous. At last, however, she realises that her aristocratic lovers are simply taking advantage of her. The unfortunate girl, now in a state of advanced pregnancy and almost penniless, agrees to the Abbess's suggestion that she should return to the convent. There Laura is delivered of her baby, her virginity is 'repaired' by the good sisters' skill in these matters, a reconciliation is effected with her parents and an advantageous marriage is arranged.)*

Letter from Madame de Merville to the Reverend Father Ignatius.

   'After two months of careful preparations, everything is at last ready for Laura's marriage: this Tuesday she will swear to her husband never to love anyone but him. Our remedy has done its work. In very truth, the most experienced libertine would take her for a maiden. Oh, how we shall laugh at the husband's expense!... He has been here three times in order to pay his respects to the young lady and has been delighted with her. It is going to be a most advantageous union and I do not doubt that the affair will be concluded to the satisfaction of all concerned.

'The community is going to lose its most amiable hussies. Sister Ursula is also getting married, and we are going to administer the same remedy to her as we did to Laura: in other words, we are going to make a *new* woman of her. Thus you have only one more opportunity of enjoying the young lady. After that the box will be sealed and it shall only be opened to the desires of her legitimate husband.

'I have something to reproach you for: you took too little care, and I find myself in the same situation as Laura: in short, I am with child.

'Come to me in all haste and compensate me by redoubling your ardour. You have nothing to fear from me but my caresses.

'Farewell, until tonight.'


Letter from Laura to Madame de Merville.

'My dearest friend,

'The deed is done! I am now Monsieur de Blainville's wife. I played my rôle so well at the critical moment that he was completely hoodwinked and enchanted by his "triumph". I screamed so loudly that our neighbours must surely have heard me. He made three attempts and was positively bathed in his own sweat. Oh, what trouble I put him to! He would swear the most solemn oath that I am the most untried of

women. If only you could have seen my embarrassment, my blushes when he desired to put his tool in my
hand, how you would have laughed! One would have
sworn that never before in my life had I set eyes upon
such a thing. He admired my breasts, my thighs, my
buttocks. All received his homage, but in spite of all
my seductive charms, I was unable to obtain a second
audience. My word, if he thinks that a young person
with a temperament as ardent as mine is going to be
satisfied with just one enjoyment, he is greatly
mistaken, and I very much fear that my virtue will
succumb to the first agreeable man who tells me that
he loves me.

'And what a difference, dear abbess, between my
husband's prick and that of our dear lamented
Bigprick! *What* a difference!

'Imagine a poor little thing, all wrinkled, with an
insignificant head, dark, flaccid balls covered in sparse
grey hairs and you have a good likeness, although
perhaps still too flattering, of the present with which
my bridegroom honoured me. Am I, who have seen
such beautiful ones, likely to be content with that? As
yet I have not dared to reveal all the fire of my
temperament to him. I am waiting upon chance to
provide me with a favourable moment.

'During the wedding festivities, my husband's
nephew caught my eye: he seems as if he may be
eminently qualified for my purpose. But he is very
young and inexperienced and I fear that it is your
humble servant who shall be obliged to make the
advances.

'Yesterday, I was introduced into society by my
husband. The very first person I set eyes upon was the

gentleman with whom I lived in Paris, and who procured me for the director of the Opera. I blushed deeply. He noticed it, and drawing near to me, said softly in my ear, "Fear nothing, lovely Laura, I shall be the soul of discretion."

'How that reassured me! I learned that he had served in the army with my husband, and that his château was not far from ours.

'Whilst the other guests were gaming or conversing, we went into the garden. He enquired by what chance I found myself the wife of his friend. I told him everything binding him to secrecy by the most solemn promise. He laughed heartily and vowed that he would break off the marriage which he was about to enter into.

'"Oh," said he, "what a lesson I have learned today!"

'He entreated me with such good grace to accord him the same favours as before that, in very truth, I could not refuse him, and we made arrangements to meet again.

'It is my intention to try to ensnare the nephew as well: in fact, I want all the men in the district for my lovers.

'I shall come and pay my respects to you soon and tell you personally about all the exciting things which have happened to me and I hope to have the pleasure of taking part in one of your orgies again.

'Now there is no longer any reason for me to fear anything: my husband is no Argus, and a woman such as myself could outwit ten thousand of them.

'Adieu, my dear abbess, adieu, my tender friend, we shall see each other frequently and I shall kiss with delight your lovely breasts. The nuptial couch awaits me, but I am not counting on experiencing very lively pleasures there. You are more fortunate than me: Brother Hercules does not neglect you.

'I send you my love, and shall always be your friend.
Laura Blainville.'

Extract from a letter to Madame de Merville from Laura.

'A miracle has occurred, my dear abbess! A miracle! My elderly husband, like some new Tithonus has become young again in his Aurora's arms: last night was more abundant in pleasures than I had dared to hope it would be. Nature caused him to make an extra effort in my behalf, and he distinguished himself no less than three times. He was delighted with my little tricks and they were marvellously effective. My husband left me this morning to go to a place some ten leagues distant. He will stay there for three days to settle some family matters.

'I did not remain a widow long: my former lover, my gentleman from Paris, came to keep me company. I acquainted him with my good fortune, telling him that my lord and master had performed his conjugal duty with honour and during that time I had quite forgotten his sixty years. When this conversation took place, we were in my bedchamber, standing close to the bed.

'He looked at it and said, "This then is the throne of your pleasures? How I envy your husband!"

'"What are you complaining about?" I said, "did you not, before him, taste those pleasures which you now seem to regret?"

'He said nothing but simply placed his hand upon

one of my breasts. Far from repulsing him, I pressed it closer to me. Emboldened by this gesture, he pushed me down upon the bed and pulled up my skirts; his burning lips kissed every part of my body.

'Once he had feasted his eyes upon my charms, he threw himself on me. I wound my legs tightly about him and wriggled my arse in perfect timing with his efforts. We both attained the moment of supreme enjoyment together. He wanted me to spend the night with him, but I would not agree to his request. It is my intention to be prudent in all my actions...'

# MORE EROTIC CLASSICS FROM CARROLL & GRAF

- [ ] Anonymous/ALTAR OF VENUS     $3.95
- [ ] Anonymous/AUTOBIOGRAPHY OF A FLEA     $3.95
- [ ] Anonymous/THE CELEBRATED MISTRESS     $3.95
- [ ] Anonymous/CONFESSIONS OF AN ENGLISH MAID     $3.95
- [ ] Anonymous/CONFESSIONS OF EVELINE     $3.95
- [ ] Anonymous/COURT OF VENUS     $3.95
- [ ] Anonymous/DANGEROUS AFFAIRS     $3.95
- [ ] Anonymous/THE DIARY OF MATA HARI     $3.95
- [ ] Anonymous/DOLLY MORTON     $3.95
- [ ] Anonymous/THE EDUCATION OF A MAIDEN     $3.95
- [ ] Anonymous/THE EROTIC READER     $3.95
- [ ] Anonymous/THE EROTIC READER II     $3.95
- [ ] Anonymous/THE EROTIC READER III     $4.50
- [ ] Anonymous/FANNY HILL'S DAUGHTER     $3.95
- [ ] Anonymous/FLORENTINE AND JULIA     $3.95
- [ ] Anonymous/A LADY OF QUALITY     $3.95
- [ ] Anonymous/LENA'S STORY     $3.95
- [ ] Anonymous/THE LIBERTINES     $4.50
- [ ] Anonymous/LOVE PAGODA     $3.95
- [ ] Anonymous/THE LUSTFUL TURK     $3.95
- [ ] Anonymous/MADELEINE     $3.95
- [ ] Anonymous/A MAID'S JOURNEY     $3.95
- [ ] Anonymous/MAID'S NIGHT IN     $3.95
- [ ] Anonymous/THE OYSTER     $3.95
- [ ] Anonymous/THE OYSTER II     $3.95
- [ ] Anonymous/THE OYSTER III     $4.50
- [ ] Anonymous/PARISIAN NIGHTS     $4.50
- [ ] Anonymous/PLEASURES AND FOLLIES     $3.95
- [ ] Anonymous/PLEASURE'S MISTRESS     $3.95
- [ ] Anonymous/PRIMA DONNA     $3.95
- [ ] Anonymous/ROSA FIELDING: VICTIM OF LUST     $3.95
- [ ] Anonymous/SATANIC VENUS     $4.50
- [ ] Anonymous/SECRET LIVES     $3.95
- [ ] Anonymous/THREE TIMES A WOMAN     $3.95

| | | |
|---|---|---|
| ☐ Anonymous/VENUS DISPOSES | | $3.95 |
| ☐ Anonymous/VENUS IN PARIS | | $3.95 |
| ☐ Anonymous/VENUS UNBOUND | | $3.95 |
| ☐ Anonymous/VENUS UNMASKED | | $3.95 |
| ☐ Anonymous/VICTORIAN FANCIES | | $3.95 |
| ☐ Anonymous/THE WANTONS | | $3.95 |
| ☐ Anonymous/A WOMAN OF PLEASURE | | $3.95 |
| ☐ Anonymous/WHITE THIGHS | | $4.50 |
| ☐ Perez, Faustino/LA LOLITA | | $3.95 |
| ☐ van Heller, Marcus/ADAM & EVE | | $3.95 |
| ☐ van Heller, Marcus/THE FRENCH WAY | | $3.95 |
| ☐ van Heller, Marcus/THE HOUSE OF BORGIA | $3.95 |
| ☐ van Heller, Marcus/THE LOINS OF AMON | $3.95 |
| ☐ van Heller, Marcus/ROMAN ORGY | | $3.95 |
| ☐ van Heller, Marcus/VENUS IN LACE | | $3.95 |
| ☐ Villefranche, Anne-Marie/FOLIES D'AMOUR | $3.95 |
|    Cloth | | $14.95 |
| ☐ Villefranche, Anne-Marie/JOIE D'AMOUR | $3.95 |
|    Cloth | | $13.95 |
| ☐ Villefranche, Anne-Marie/ MYSTERE | | |
|    D'AMOUR | | $3.95 |
| ☐ Villefranche, Anne-Marie/PLAISIR D'AMOUR | $3.95 |
|    Cloth | | $12.95 |
| ☐ Von Falkensee, Margarete/BLUE ANGEL | | |
|    NIGHTS | | $3.95 |
| ☐ Von Falkensee, Margarete/BLUE ANGEL | | |
|    SECRETS | | $4.50 |

Available from fine bookstores everywhere or use this coupon for ordering.

---

Carroll & Graf Publishers, Inc., 260 Fifth Avenue, N.Y., N.Y. 10001

Please send me the books I have checked above. I am enclosing
$_____ (please add $1.00 per title to cover postage and
handling.) Send check or money order—no cash or C.O.D.'s
please. N.Y. residents please add 8¼% sales tax.

Mr/Mrs/Ms _____
Address _____
City _____ State/Zip _____
Please allow four to six weeks for delivery.